Anonymous

Gems

Anonymous

Gems

ISBN/EAN: 9783337303099

Printed in Europe, USA, Canada, Australia, Japan

Cover: Foto ©Andreas Hilbeck / pixelio.de

More available books at **www.hansebooks.com**

Streeter & Co. Ltd.

18 New Bond St. London W.

STREETER & Co. Ltd. in issuing their hundredth and one BOOK, beg to state that only Gems of fine quality are used in the manufacture of their goods, and all stones being set *à jour*, no foil or enamel is employed, unless where specially ordered The Company's position in the jewellery trade is unrivalled, Mr. STREETER, under whose personal supervision the business is managed, possessing a complete knowledge of every detail necessary for ensuring success, and having the advantage of connections throughout the Gem-producing countries of the world.

The prices quoted in this Catalogue are based upon the lowest possible margin of profit, in fact, the Directors confidently assert that, quality considered, no other firm can conscientiously undersell them. Being interested in the different Gem Mines, and buying all other precious stones in the rough for cash (which are cut by specially engaged Lapidaries) each article is manufactured by highly skilled craftsmen in their own workshops, thereby placing the purchaser in direct communication with the actual producer, and saving all intermediate profits.

Intending purchasers not finding herein articles to meet their particular requirements can, by furnishing a London reference, have an assortment of Jewels from the finest and one of the largest stocks in London, sent to their residences for approval, without any charge or risk to themselves. as the Company insure with *Lloyd's* all goods in transit each way. Foreign and Colonial Customers desirous of leaving the selection to the firm may rely on their wishes being faithfully carried out, it being the Directors' endeavour to maintain the high uniform standard of excellence for which this firm has been noted for more than two centuries.

The Directors of STREETER & Co. specially invite those who take an interest in gems to visit the Museum in the *atelier* at New Bond Street, where specimens of every known gem, both in the rough and cut, may be seen. From this collection, unique in its kind, purchasers may choose their own stones and have them set under their personal direction and to their own design. Collections of Precious Stones and Gems, in the rough or cut, arranged to order from £5 to £5,000.

It may not be out of place to take this opportunity of devoting a few words to the subject of Pearls. These products of Nature stand pre-eminent in the ranks of precious gems, and so rarely are Pearls of perfect quality and symmetry found that they rapidly increase in value. To those who are possessors of these gems, Mr. STREETER wishes to announce that he has invented a process by which many old and discoloured Pearls can be successfully restored to their original lustre, and their value enhanced thereby.

A short description of the most important Gem Stones (being extracts from Mr. Streeter's work on Precious Stones and Gems) has been added, with the hope that they may prove of interest.

Regimental Souvenirs, Badges, Bowls, Cups, Enamelled Racing and Yachting Colors and Models, also Hunting Buttons, a speciality. The Directors having the benefit of the advice of an authority on this subject, the possibility of mistake in device or colouring is entirely removed

Valuation of Gems, Jewellery and Silver made for probate, or to purchase, and if desired, Mr. STREETER will undertake the division of family jewels according to their proportionate value.

Cheques and Postal Orders payable to STREETER & Co. crossed "London & County Bank," Hanover Square Branch, W.

Correspondence cordially invited from every part of the World on any subject concerning Pearls, Gems, and Semi-Precious Stones.

18, NEW BOND STREET,
        LONDON, W.

THE DIAMOND.

HE crystalline forms in which the Diamond occurs in nature belong to the group of geometrical solids known to crystallographers as the Cubic or Tesseral, or Isometric system. The surface of a crystal of Diamond is generally smooth; but it is sometimes indented with triangular impressions, and in certain cases is striated with lines parallel to the edges of the faces. Some Diamonds present a rough surface, resembling a poorly polished glass, and are not unfrequently dull, as though covered with a thin coating of gum. The Diamond presents a perfect cleavage parallel to the faces of the octahedron, which is its primary form. The Diamond cutter avails himself of his knowledge of this natural structure, and is thereby enabled in many cases to remove spots from a stone by cleaving, without resorting to the weary work of grinding. In addition to the property of cleavage, the Diamond possesses pre-eminently that of hardness, a quality in which it so exceeds all other bodies that it can penetrate them without being itself even scratched. The conditions which the Diamond presents in relation to light are very remarkable. It is one of those bodies which refract light most strongly, that is to say, when a ray of light enters a Diamond, it is turned from its original path to a much greater extent than if it had entered a Topaz, or a Rock Crystal, or a piece of glass, or, in fact, any other transparent medium. In addition to this property it also possesses the power in an extraordinary degree of reflecting and dispersing the rays of light, thus causing what is technically termed the " play of colors," observable on a well-cut Diamond. The optical term, dispersion, is applied to the power which a transparent substance possesses of breaking up the incident white light into prismatic tints, like those of the rainbow, a power which is enjoyed to an unusual extent by the Diamond, and gives rise to the splendid flashes of fire emitted by a stone that has been skilfully cut. The Diamond in its purest condition is colourless and transparent, yet at times it is found coloured throughout of almost every possible tint. The colours ranging from bright canary yellow to a deep brown and black, and in very rare instances green, blue, pink and red ; these latter tints are highly valued as fancy stones.

The Diamond is a non-conductor of electricity, a fact

which is the more remarkable as Graphite or Charcoal, substances absolutely identical with it chemically, are very good conductors. By friction, however, both in the rough and polished state, it becomes positively electric, but loses its electricity completely in the course of half-an-hour. When exposed to the intense heat of the electric arc, the Diamond swells up, becomes black, and is converted superficially into a substance resembling Graphite. Diamonds are found in India, Sumatra, Borneo, Brazil and South Africa, parts of North America, British Guiana, the Ural Mountains, and Australia. Other countries have been pointed out, but confirmatory evidence of the truth of this assertion is required.

A remarkable discovery has recently been made which has invested the Diamond with an interest even greater than it could previously claim. Scientists in submitting certain meteorites or sky-stones to a careful examination have found in some of them carbon in a diamontoid condition. It is true that this carbon was rather of the character of carbonado, the black variety of Diamond ; but still the presence of any kind of Diamond in an ærolite is a fact of surpassing scientific interest.

Composition ...	*Pure Carbon.*
Specific gravity ...	3.52 *to* 3.53.
Hardness	10.
System of Crystallization	*Isometric or cubical.*
Common forms of Crystal ...	*Octahedron, Rhombic Dodecahedron, Hexakis, Octahedron, etc.*

THE RUBY.

HE Ruby not only stands in the very foremost class of coloured gems, but it occupies among precious stones in general a position which is unquestionably supreme. By the ancients it was regarded as the very type of all that was most precious in the natural world ; and its value is amply attested by the numerous allusions to it in the Old Testament.

Before mineralogy became a science, and could call to its aid the services of chemistry and physics, it was by no means surprising that various stones of red colour should be confounded together; thus the Spinel or Balas and the Garnet were often mistaken for the true Ruby. The only stone, however, to which the term Ruby can in scientific strictness be applied is a variety of the mineral-species termed Corundum. The crystals of Corundum are often ill-shaped and rough, and usually much rolled. The lustre of Corundum is vitreous, but sometimes pearly on the basal planes, and the crystals, when properly cut, occasionally exhibit a bright opalescent star of six rays in the direction of the principal axis. Such crystals form the star stone. The refractive index of Corundum is 1.77, and therefore higher than that of glass ; hence the great brilliancy of the Corundum gem stones, when properly cut and polished. All varieties of Corundum can be scratched by the Diamond, but by no other mineral. Although Corundum is a mineral which, in its various forms, enjoys a fairly wide geographical distribution, it is remarkable that the fine red varieties are extremely rare and restricted in their occurrence. The localities yielding the Rubies of commerce are indeed practically limited to Burmah, Siam and Ceylon. Even of these localities it is only Burmah that has acquired celebrity for the favourite tint, the true pigeon's-blood colour ; those of Siam being generally too dark, and those of Ceylon too pale, to satisfy the connoisseur, though in both places a fine gem is occasionally found. The price paid for this stone by the ancients was very high. According to Benvenuto Cellini, in his time a perfect Ruby of a carat weight cost 800 ecus d'or, whilst a Diamond of like weight cost only 100 ; the same applies to-day, for the Ruby ranks in price above all other stones. When a perfect Ruby of five carats is brought into the market a sum will be offered for it ten times the price given for a

Diamond of the same weight ; but should it reach the weight of ten carats or more it is almost invaluable. A fine stone may have its value considerably depreciated by injudicious cutting, as is generally done in the East by native lapidaries ; apart from the question of workmanship (which it is well known is inferior), the Indian and European systems are so utterly opposed that the result must be a loss either of weight or beauty. The native cuts for weight only, without the least regard for either brilliancy or shape ; whereas, on the other hand, the English lapidary cuts for brilliancy and colour even at the sacrifice of weight. In a perfect shaped stone the front, *i.e*, that part that is above the girdle, should be one-third, and the back two-thirds of the total thickness of the stone ; experience shows that these proportions give the best effect. The author has devoted many years to the perfecting of the cutting of precious stones and has established a laboratory where stones, either in the rough or cut, are worked. Owners of precious stones are cordially invited to consult him as to the advisability of having their gems re-cut or re-polished, thereby often much enhancing their brilliancy and value.

Composition	...	*Alumina.*
Specific gravity ...		4.
Hardness		9, *or slightly under.*
System of Crystallization	...	*Hexagonal.*
Form ...	... ...	*Six-sided prisms and pyra-mids, variously modified, but usually as rolled fragments.*

THE SAPPHIRE.

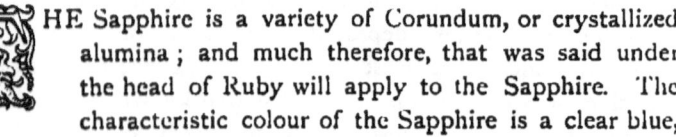HE Sapphire is a variety of Corundum, or crystallized alumina; and much therefore, that was said under the head of Ruby will apply to the Sapphire. The characteristic colour of the Sapphire is a clear blue, very like that of the blossom of the little "Cornflower," and the more velvety its appearance, the greater its value. Some Sapphires retain their colour by gaslight, while others become dark, and some assume a reddish or purple colour, and occasionally have the hue of the Amethyst. While the typical colour of the Sapphire is blue, it should be explained that the term "Sapphire" is extended by mineralogists and jewellers to Corundums of other colours. Thus, we have green Sapphires, various shades of yellow and grey, while others again may be entirely destitute of colour; these pure white Sapphires being sometimes mistaken, when skilfully cut, for Diamonds. The principal Sapphire yielding localities now worked are in Siam, Burmah, Cashmere, and Ceylon. The Sapphires of Siam are the finest at present in the market; the mines in Cashmere have yielded some very fine stones, but the great majority are only of a pale greyish blue. Large deposits of Sapphire have been found in Montana, but the stones are mostly of green and other fancy tints, and not deep blue. A remarkable characteristic of the Montana stones is their great brilliancy when cut, almost rivalling that of the Diamond.

Sapphires are also known to occur in Borneo, Madagascar, the Ural Mountains, and several other localities. In Europe they are found on the Iser, in Bohemia; in the Sieben-Gebirge, on the Rhine; in Saxony; and in France, notably at Expailly, near Le Puy-en-Valey. The European Sapphires, however, are only of scientific interest to the mineralogist, and of no commercial value.

Many large crystals of Sapphire have been found in Australia, but they are of such a dark inky blue colour, in some cases being almost opaque, that they are of little value as Precious Stones. The value of these stones is very much determined by special circumstances, and, like the Diamond, the colour, purity, and size must be taken into consideration when fixing the sum to be paid. A perfect Oriental Sapphire, weighing between two and three carats, is nearly as costly as a good Diamond of like weight

The imperfections which appear at times in the Sapphire, and which lessen its value, are clouds, milky half-opaque spots, white glassy stripes, rents, knots, a congregating of colour at one spot, and silky-looking flakes on the table of the stone. Varieties of the "Doublet" are made of the Sapphire as well as of the Ruby and other gems ; these consist of thin layers of true stone facing crystal, so as to appear but one stone. They may be distinguished from the genuine stone partly by their colour, but more especially by a careful examination of the girdle, when the join may usually be readily detected. Notwithstanding the extreme hardness of the Sapphire there are some beautifully engraved specimens of this gem in existence. In the cabinet of Strozzi, in Rome, is a Sapphire, a masterpiece of art, with the profile of Hercules engraved on it by Cnevus. A very remarkable and famous Sapphire, belonging to the Marchese Rinuccini, weighing fifty-three carats, has a representation of a hunting scene engraven upon it, with the inscription "Constantius Aug." Among a number of old family jewels there was found by the author, some few years ago, a Sapphire beautifully engraved with the crest and arms of Cardinal Wolsey.

Composition	*Alumina.*
Specific gravity	4. *or slightly under.*
Hardness	9.
System of Crystallization ...	*Hexagonal.*
Form	*Double six-sided pyramids,*
	or prisms ; usually as rolled crystals.

THE EMERALD.

HE Emerald, from a mineralogist's point of view, belongs to a class of stones altogether different from that which embraces the precious stones already described, inasmuch as it is essentially a mineral silicate, consisting largely of the substance known to chemists as silica. The silica is itself an oxide of an element termed silicon, which is closely related in many ways to carbon. In the Emerald the silica is combined with the oxides of two metals—one of them being aluminium, the basis of the Ruby and Sapphire; while the other is an exceedingly rare metal, known as glucinum or beryllium. Just as it was shown that the Ruby and the Sapphire are identical, save in colour, so the chemist has found that the Emerald, the Beryl, and the Aquamarine are practically the same mineral, the distinctions between the three varieties being due to differences of colour and other characteristics of only trivial value to the chemist, though of immense importance to the jeweller as affecting their commercial value. The Emerald is found crystallized in six-sided prisms or columns, without striations, and, therefore, unlike those of Beryl, and without any inclination to the cylindrical form. The colour varies from what is called emerald-green, to grass-green, and greenish-white. The variety of opinion as to the source of the beautiful colour of the Emerald is very interesting, but, according to most authorities, it owes its beauty to the chromium which it contains. It is doubtful if Emeralds have ever been found in India; though they are sent there, in the rough, from other localities, and after having been cut in India, are forwarded to this country for sale. It is said that, in Burmah, Emeralds have from time to time been picked out of the sand or beds of small rivers. In the treasure from Mandalay, now in the South Kensington Museum, are some very large Emeralds, but they are probably from South America.

The Ural and Altai Mountains have of late years furnished true Emeralds. Very fine crystals of Emerald are found in mica-schist at Stretnisk, on the River Takowja, which lies to the north of Katherinenburg, on the Asiatic slope of the Urals. The mineral also occurs in the Mountains of the Sahara, in beds of mica-slate; and in the bed of the River Harrach, in Algeria, where it joins the River Oned Bouman. Emeralds have been recorded from several localities in New South Wales, but they are rare, and usually of no commercial value.

The most famous Emerald mines of the world are those of Muzo, about 75 miles N.N.W. of Santa Fé de Bogata, in the Republic of Columbia. They were discovered by Lanchero in 1555, but the Spaniards did not commence working until 1568. In Eastern Egypt too, at Sikait and Jebel Zabbara, Emeralds have been mined for from time immemorial, these being probably the earliest known Emerald mines in the world. The Emeralds of Egypt have often been mentioned with high praise. Cleopatra gave, as presents to ambassadors, portraits of herself engraved on Emeralds, and the stones during her reign appear to have been considered as strictly royal property. The value of an Emerald depends greatly upon its colour and freedom from flaws; a very fine dark velvety coloured stone, free from flaw, is seldom procurable. Perhaps there is no stone which suffers more than the Emerald from inequality of structure, colour and transparency, and from clouds and spots.

Composition	...	...	...	Silica	..	68
				Alumina	...	18
				Glucina, &c.		14
						100

Specific gravity ... ... 2.7.
Hardness ... ... 7.5.
System .. .. Hexagonal.
Form ... ... *Hexagonal and di-hexagonal prisms, variously modified.*

THE ORIENTAL CAT'S-EYE.

MUCH confusion exists concerning this very curious and valuable gem, a confusion arising partly from the ignorance of many in the trade as to its true nature, but principally from the mistakes of those who have written about it. In mineralogical treatises it is often confounded with, and described as, a peculiar variety of quartz, which somewhat resembles it, but which is of little or no mercantile value, although it has occasionally been sent to Europe by unscrupulous merchants as the true Cat's-Eye. This chatoyant quartz is found largely in Ceylon and on the West Coast of India. A greenish variety is found near Hof, in Bavaria, and is largely cut as an ornamental stone. The quartz Cat's-Eye is semi-transparent, and when cut in a convex form (*en cabochon*) shows a more or less defined band of light, with a silky lustre, resulting from a reflection of the fibrous grain of the stone itself, or more probably from an intimate admixture of asbestos, which penetrates the quartz in delicate parallel fibres. The true or Oriental Cat's-Eye is a rare variety of the Chrysoberyl, or Cymophane, a stone of extreme hardness, in this respect being only inferior to the Diamond and the Sapphire. It is characterized by possessing a remarkable play of light in a certain direction, resulting it is supposed from a peculiarity in its internal structure, which appears to be minutely striated. This ray of light or "line" as it is termed by jewellers, shines in fine and well-polished specimens with a phosphorescent lustre. The true Cat's-Eye (Chrysoberyl) comes principally from Ceylon, where it is found in company with Sapphires, Zircons, and other gem-stones. It is of various colours, ranging from pale-straw colour through all shades of brown, and from very pale apple-green to the deepest olive. Some specimens are almost black. The line, no matter what ground-colour the stone may possess, is nearly always white, and more or less iridescent; occasionally, but very rarely, however, the line is of a golden-hue. This lustre is most beautiful when seen in full sun-light or by gas-light, when the lines become more defined and vivid. This gem is valued principally according to the perfection and brilliancy of the luminous line, which should be sharp and well-defined, not very broad, and should run evenly from end to end across the middle of the stone. The colour does not much influence the value, some jewellers preferring one tint and some another. On the whole, perhaps, the most popular colours are the clear apple-green and dark olive ; both of these form a splendid background and contrast well with the line. A great deal of so-called Cat's-Eye was, some few years back, brought from South Africa, and, mounted as jewellery in various forms, was sold as African Cat's-Eye ; it is however merely a fibrous form of quartz, known generally as " Crocidolite." This African Cat's-Eye, or Crocidolite, has been brought from Griqualand in masses of suffi- cient size to be made into snuff-boxes and other ornamental objects ; while slabs of the stone have been used as veneer to cover the tops of small tables.

It will have been gathered from the foregoing remarks, that no fewer than four different stones are known under the name of Cat's-Eye, namely :—

(1) The fibrous variety of Chrysoberyl.
(2) The chatoyant quartz from India.
(3) The green asbestiferous variety from Bavaria.
(4) The brown " Crocidolite " from South Africa.

But it must be borne in mind that the only one as a gem of real value is that which has been described above as the true or Oriental Cat's-Eye—a fibrous variety of Chrysoberyl—far surpassing in hardness and beauty any of its namesakes.

Composition	*Alumina* ... 80.
	Glucina ... 20.
	——
	100
Specific gravity ...	3.8
Hardness	8.5
System	*Trimetric.*
Form	*Usually as rolled crystals.*

THE OPAL.

ICOLS in his curious old book entitled " A Lapidary," written two centuries and a half ago, gives a quaint description of this lovely stone. He says:—" The Opal is a Precious Stone which hath in it the bright, fiery flame of the Carbuncle, the fine, refulgent purple of an Amethyst, and a whole sea of the Emerald's green glory ; and every one of them shining with an incredible mixture and very much pleasure." In all notices of the Opal, prominence is naturally given to the brilliant play of rainbow tints which renders this stone unique. Although possessing no colour which can properly be called its own, it exhibits flashes of the most vivid hues. This is probably the result of the number of fissures which traverse it, the light being decomposed by the delicate striations on the walls of these microscopic crevices, thus giving rise to the optical phenomena known as " diffraction." In some varieties the colours are more or less evenly distributed, and one set of shades will predominate in one part of the stone, and other colours in another part ; or the distinct tints will run in parallel bands. In other specimens the colours are made up of small regular angular patches of every hue, and these polychromatic stones are known as Harlequin Opals.

The Opal is a non-crystalline mineral. When first taken out of the earth it is not very hard, but subsequently by exposure to the air its hardness is increased ; nevertheless, it always remains a soft stone compared with other gems.

Several kinds of Opal are known to the mineralogist. Most of it is destitute of brilliancy, and hence useless to the jeweller. This is known as common Opal. Other specimens present translucency, but no colour ; these are distinguished as Semi-Opal. Certain Opals from Zimapan, in Mexico, possess a bright orange-red tint, and are used to a limited extent as an ornamental stone under the name of Fire-Opal. The Precious Opal, used in bijouterie, was formerly obtained almost exclusively from Hungary, the mountain range where it was found consisting mainly of a kind of trachytic rock, or porphyritic andesite. The two highest mountains of this range are Simonka and Libanka, and it is from these that the Precious Opal came, especially from Dubrick. There seems no doubt that the Opal mass, originally in a liquid or gelatinous condition, filled up the cavities in the trachyte veins and was gradually solidified. The Mexican Opal occurs at several localities, and is also found in Honduras, in the Department of Gracias, and in Guatemala. Most of this Central American Opal is more transparent and less fiery than that from Hungary, and with the exception of a few isolated specimens is considered of but little value. Of late years large quantities of Precious Opal has been found in Queensland, and also in New South Wales, occurring principally in thin veins in brown ironstone. Owing to the exhaustion of the Hungarian mines Australia has now become the principal source from which jewellers obtain this beautiful stone; it is somewhat of a more transparent character than the Hungarian Opal, but many of the finer pieces equal in beauty and brilliancy of colouring the choicest specimens from Hungary. It is well known that there are innumerable superstitions attached to the Opal. By the ancients it was thought to bestow every possible good. In the Middle Ages the same belief was held ; but by a strange freak of fashion the Opal lost its pristine glory, and for a long time has been falsely accused of bringing ill-luck—a bad reputation which the author is glad to say is now almost entirely removed. Sir Walter Scott is said to be in a great measure answerable for this, as readers of *Anne of Geierstein* know. The Opal is a favourite stone with the Queen, the German Royal Family, and with many of our aristocracy. The Americans have also of late years shown a marked partiality for the stone, thousands of carats of the finest stones having been purchased for their market.

Composition ...	*Silica, with* 10 *to* 12 *per cent. Water.*
Specific gravity	2 *to* 2.2
Hardness	5.5 *to* 6.
Form	*Amorphous.*

THE ALEXANDRITE.

HIS stone, which was named after the late Czar of Russia, having been discovered on the birthday of Alexander I., owes its celebrity to its prominent hues of red and green. The Russian Alexandrite can rarely be shown to the best advantage in consequence of its radical defects of structure. The variety found in Ceylon is more easy of manipulation.

Alexandrite is especially remarkable for its strongly-marked difference of colour, according as it is viewed by natural or by artificial light. The finest stones present a bright green, or deep olive-green colour, by daylight ; whereas at night artificial light, such as that of gas or a candle, brings out a soft columbine red or raspberry tint. The Alexandrite is strongly dichroic, while some varieties are even trichroic.

Chemical analysis shows that the Alexandrite is a variety of Chrysoberyl. The author has seen in the course of his experience two or three stones with a perfect Cat's-Eye line, yet subject to the characteristic change of colour by artificial light ; such stones are called Alexandrite Cat's-Eyes. In order to display the line of light, it is necessary to cut the stone *en cabochon* instead of facetting it. The original Alexandrite came from the Ural Mountains only in small quantities ; but the principal supply now is obtained from Ceylon, where, however, it is far from plentiful. The market value of this stone is extremely variable.

Composition :—

Alumina	79
Glucina	18
Iron and Chromic oxide, &c.	3
	100

Specific gravity ...	3.7.
Hardness	... 8.5.
System of Crystallization	... *Trimetric.*
Form of Crystal ...	... *Usually six-sided twins.*

1002

1001

1003

1004

1005

1006

1007

1008

1009

1010

The £5 5s. Jewel page.

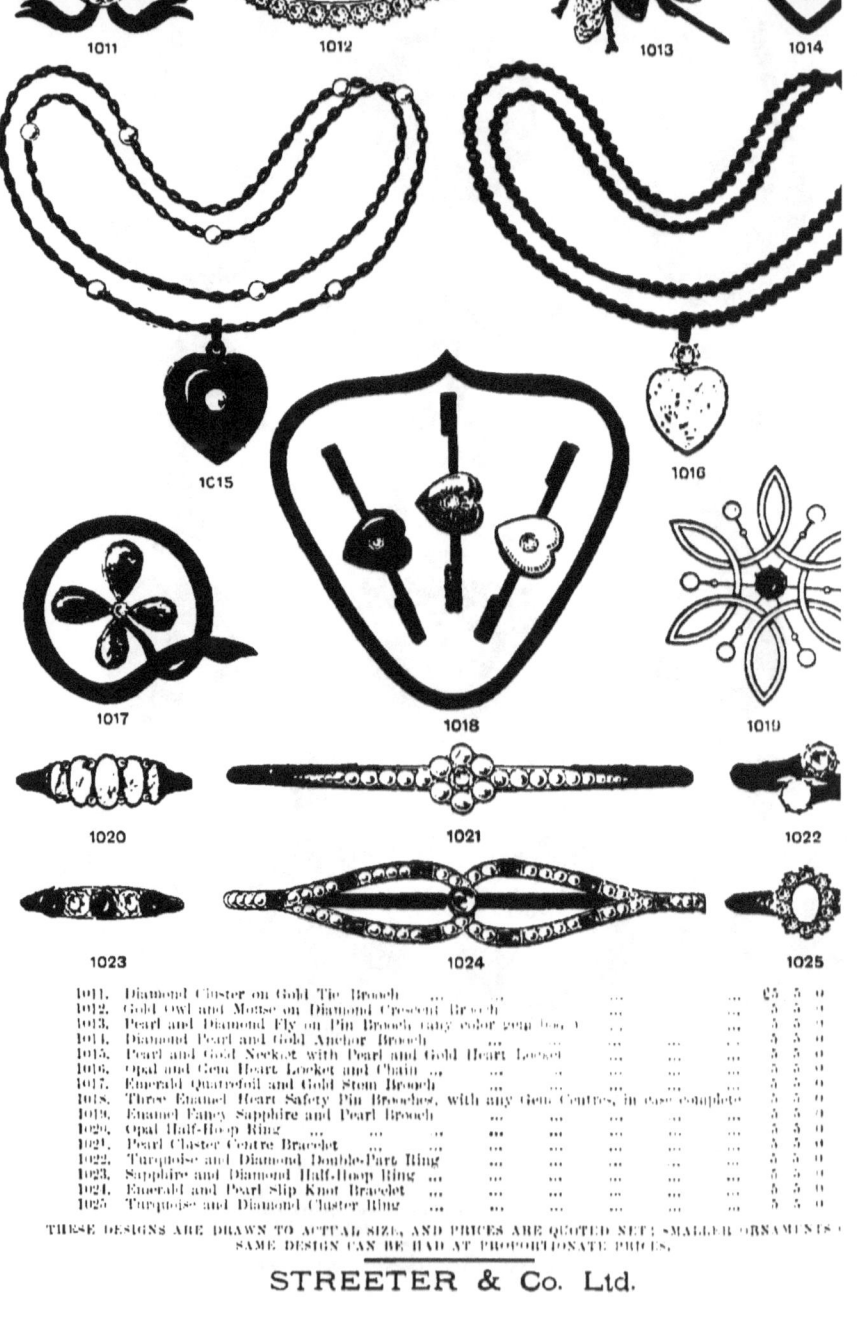

1011   1012   1013   1014

1015   1016

1017   1018   1019

1020   1021   1022

1023   1024   1025

1011.	Diamond Cluster on Gold Tie Brooch	...	...			...	£5 5 0
1012.	Gold Owl and Mouse on Diamond Crescent Brooch			...		...	5 5 0
1013.	Pearl and Diamond Fly on Pin Brooch (any color you like)		...			...	5 5 0
1014.	Diamond Pearl and Gold Anchor Brooch	...	...		...	...	5 5 0
1015.	Pearl and Gold Necket with Pearl and Gold Heart Locket		...	...	...	...	5 5 0
1016.	Opal and Gem Heart Locket and Chain ...	...	...	...	...	...	5 5 0
1017.	Emerald Quatrefoil and Gold Stem Brooch	...	...	...	...	...	5 5 0
1018.	Three Enamel Heart Safety Pin Brooches, with any Gem Centres, in case complete						5 5 0
1019.	Enamel Fancy Sapphire and Pearl Brooch	...	...	...	...	...	5 5 0
1020.	Opal Half-Hoop Ring ...	...	...	...	...	...	...	5 5 0
1021.	Pearl Cluster Centre Bracelet	...	...	•••	•••	...	5 5 0
1022.	Turquoise and Diamond Double-Part Ring	...	...	...	...	...	5 5 0
1023.	Sapphire and Diamond Half-Hoop Ring ...	...	...	...	...	...	5 5 0
1024.	Emerald and Pearl Slip Knot Bracelet	...	...	...	...	...	5 5 0
1025.	Turquoise and Diamond Cluster Ring	...	•••	...	...	...	5 5 0

THESE DESIGNS ARE DRAWN TO ACTUAL SIZE, AND PRICES ARE QUOTED SET; SMALLER ORNAMENTS
SAME DESIGN CAN BE HAD AT PROPORTIONATE PRICES.

STREETER & Co. Ltd.

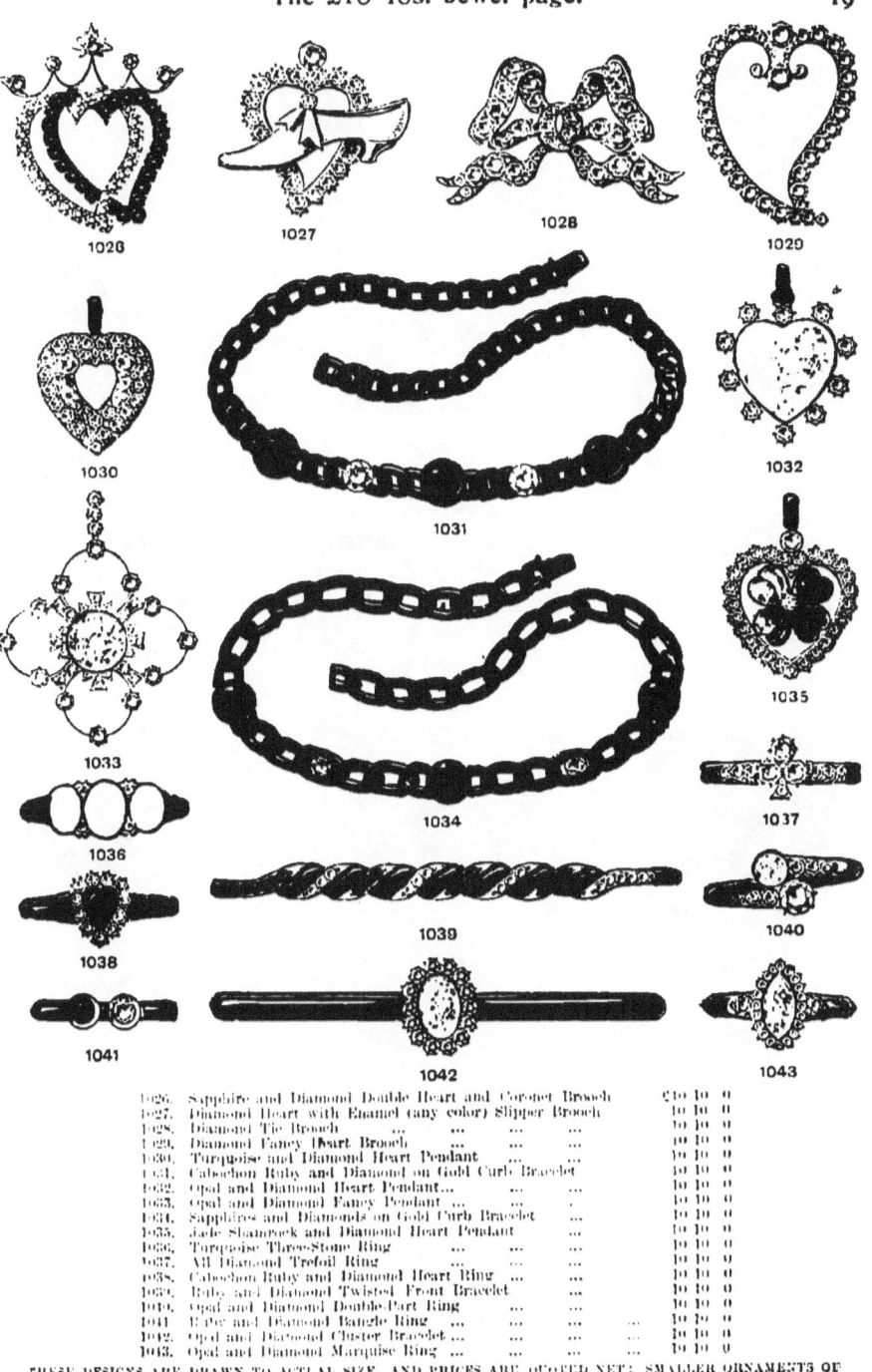

1044	1045	1046
1047	1048	1049
1050	1051	1052
1053	1054	1055
1056	1057	1058

1044.	Diamond Trefoil Brooch	...	...	...	...	...	£40	0 0
1045.	Diamond Anchor Brooch	...	...	...	...	...	35	0 0
1046.	Diamond Fancy Trefoil Brooch	...	...	...	...	45	0 0
1047.	Diamond Heart and Ribbon Brooch	...	...	...	20	0 0
1048.	Diamond Fancy Crescent Brooch	...	...	...	...	35	0 0
1049.	Turquoise and Diamond Double Heart and Tie Brooch	...	55	0 0
1050.	Turquoise and Diamond Oval Cluster Brooch	...	...	65	0 0
1051.	Diamond Double Crescent and Tie Brooch	...	...	35	0 0
1052.	Pearl and Diamond "Tara" Brooch	...	...	...	25	0 0
1053.	Sapphire and Diamond Three Crescent and Star Brooch	...	65	0 0
1054.	Emerald and Diamond Butterfly Brooch	...	...	50	0 0
1055.	Pearl and Diamond Snake and Arrow Brooch	...	...	40	0 0
1056.	Pearl and Diamond Crescent on Bar Brooch	...	...	10	0 0
1057.	Sapphire and Diamond Double Heart and Tie Brooch	...	70	0 0
1058.	Sapphire and Diamond Bar Brooch	...	...	...	30	0 0

THESE DESIGNS ARE DRAWN TO ACTUAL SIZE, AND PRICES ARE QUOTED NET; SMALLER ORNAMENTS OF SAME DESIGN CAN BE HAD AT PROPORTIONATE PRICES.

STREETER & Co. Ltd.

1059

1060

1061

1062

1063

1064

1065

1067

1068

1068

1069

1070

1071

1072

1073

1059.	Sapphire and Diamond Cluster Brooch	...	...	...	£100	0	0
1060.	Diamond Butterfly Brooch	...	...	...	110	0	0
1061.	Colored Pearl and Diamond Four Leaf Shamrock Brooch	...			85	0	0
1062.	Diamond Antique Pattern Brooch	...	...	...	60	0	0
1063.	Ruby and Diamond Double Row Crescent Brooch	...		...	45	0	0
1064.	Diamond Crescent and Comet Brooch	...	...	...	34	0	0
1065.	Diamond Antique Brooch	...	...	...	...	25	0	0
1066.	Pearl and Diamond Spider and Web Brooch (half size £20)				35	0	0
1067.	Pink, Black and White Pearl and Diamond Brooch	...			40	0	0
1068.	Pearl and Diamond Twist Knot Brooch	...	...	...	18	0	0
1069.	Sapphire and Diamond Half-Moon Brooch	...	...	...	35	0	0
1070.	Ruby and Diamond Horse Shoe Brooch	...	...	...	40	0	0
1071.	Opal and Diamond Heart on Bar Brooch	...	...	...	15	0	0
1072.	Opal and Diamond Fancy Bar Brooch	...	...	...	12	10	0
1073.	Opal and Diamond Fancy Bar Brooch	...	...	...	6	15	0

THESE DESIGNS ARE DRAWN TO ACTUAL SIZE, AND PRICES ARE QUOTED NET; SMALLER ORNAMENTS OF
SAME DESIGN CAN BE HAD AT PROPORTIONATE PRICES.

18, New Bond Street, W.

1074

1075

1076

1077

1078

1079

1080

1081

1082

1083

1084

1085

1086

1087

1088

1074.	Diamond Pomeranian Dog Brooch	£25 0 0
1075.	Diamond Deer Brooch	22 0 0
1076.	Diamond Dachshund Brooch ...	22 0 0
1077.	Diamond Hackney Brooch	25 0 0
1078.	Diamond Otter Brooch	35 0 0
1079.	Diamond Woodcock Brooch	9 10 0
1080.	Diamond and Enamel Golf Player Brooch ..	15 0 0
1081.	Diamond Bicycle Brooch	22 0 0
1082.	Diamond Owl Brooch	22 0 0
1083.	Diamond Donkey Brooch	35 0 0
1084.	Diamond Lucky Pig Brooch	45 0 0
1085.	Diamond Running Fox Brooch	30 0 0
1086.	Diamond Polo Pony with Enamel Rider Brooch ..	25 0 0
1087.	Diamond and Enamel Hansom Cab Brooch ...	12 0 0
1088.	Diamond Collie Dog Brooch	35 0 0

THESE DESIGNS ARE DRAWN TO ACTUAL SIZE, AND PRICES ARE QUOTED NET; SMALLER ORNAMENTS OF
SAME DESIGN CAN BE HAD AT PROPORTIONATE PRICES.

STREETER & Co. Ltd.

(ANY COLOURED GEMS CUT
AND MOUNTED IN THE COACH BODY TO ORDER).

1089

1090   'ANY COLOURS ENAMELLED TO ORDER).

1091

1092

1093   **1094**   **1095**

1096   **1097**   **1098**

1089.	Sapphire, Ruby and Diamond Four-in-Hand Coach, Diamond Horses, Coach of Gems—Sapphires and Rubies	£80	0	0
1090.	Diamond Cat Brooch	40	0	0
1091.	Diamond Race Horse with Enamel Jockey Brooch	48	0	0
1092.	Diamond Snipe Brooch	17	0	0
1093.	Diamond Pheasant Brooch	17	0	0
1094.	Diamond Horse's Head and Horse Shoe Brooch	50	0	0
1095.	Diamond Black-cock Brooch	30	0	0
1096.	Diamond Hare Brooch	35	0	0
1097.	Diamond and Gold Poodle Brooch	16	0	0
1098.	Diamond Pug Dog Brooch	35	0	0

THESE DESIGNS ARE DRAWN TO ACTUAL SIZE, AND PRICES ARE QUOTED NET; SMALLER ORNAMENTS OF
SAME DESIGN CAN BE HAD AT PROPORTIONATE PRICES.

18, New Bond Street, W.

No.	Description			£	s	d
1099.	Diamond Fancy Pattern Bracelet	...	...	£42	0	0
1100.	Turquoise and Diamond Heart and Tie Bracelet...			55	0	0
1101.	Sapphire and Diamond Greek Key Bracelet		...	85	0	0
1102.	Emerald and Diamond Fancy Cluster Bracelet		...	45	0	0
1103.	Pearl and Diamond Fancy Bracelet	...	...	55	0	0
1104.	Cat's-eye and Diamond Cluster Bracelet	...	...	52	10	0
1105.	Opal and Diamond Cluster Bracelet	...	...	50	0	0
1106.	Diamond Three-Row Bracelet	...	...	155	0	0
1107.	Diamond Scroll Bracelet	...	...	47	10	0
1108.	Pearl and Diamond Half-Hoop Bracelet	...	...	80	0	0
1109.	Sapphire and Diamond Cluster Bracelet	...	...	58	0	0
1110.	Fine Diamond Half-Hoop Bracelet	...	...	120	0	0

THESE DESIGNS ARE DRAWN TO ACTUAL SIZE, AND PRICES ARE QUOTED NET; SMALLER ORNAMENTS OF SAME DESIGN CAN BE HAD AT PROPORTIONATE PRICES,

STREETER & Co. Ltd

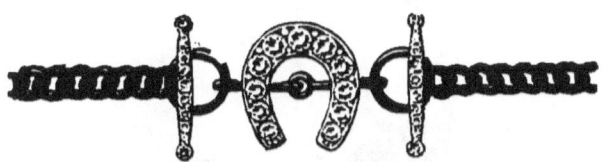

1111

1112

1113

1114

1115

1116

1117

1118

1119

1111.	Diamond Snaffle Bit and Horse Shoe on Gold Curb Bracelet ...	£12 10	0
1112.	Cat's-eye and Diamond Three-Cluster on Gold Curb Bracelet ...	35 0	0
1113.	Sapphire and Diamond Scroll and Gold Curb Bracelet	45 0	0
1114.	Pearl and Diamond alternate on Gold Curb Bracelet ...	35 0	0
1115.	Turquoise and Diamond Fancy Flexible Bracelet	50 0	0
1116.	Diamond Heart and Cluster Flexible Bracelet	180 0	0
1117.	Ruby and Diamond alternate on Gold Curb Bracelet	26 0	0
1118.	Opal and Diamond Heart and Tie Bracelet	28 0	0
1119.	Pearl and Diamond Collet on Gold Curb Bracelet	65 0	0

THESE DESIGNS ARE DRAWN TO ACTUAL SIZE, AND PRICES ARE QUOTED NET; SMALLER ORNAMENTS OF
SAME DESIGN CAN BE HAD AT PROPORTIONATE PRICES.

18, New Bond Street, W.

STREETER & Co. Ltd.

1129

1130

1131

1132   1133   1134   1135   1136

1137   1138   1139

1129.
1130. } Fine Diamond Riviere Necklaces, from £100 up-
1131.)   wards, according to size.

1132.
1133.
1134. } Fine Diamond Single Stone Earrings, from £20
1135.   upwards, according to size.
1136.

1137. Pair Pearl and Diamond Cluster Earrings   ...   £35 0 0
1138. Pair Turquoise and Diamond Cluster Earrings ...   30 0 0
1139. Pair Sapphire and Diamond Cluster Earrings ...   30 0 0

THESE DESIGNS ARE DRAWN TO ACTUAL SIZE, AND PRICES ARE QUOTED NET ; SMALLER ORNAMENTS OF
SAME DESIGN CAN BE HAD AT PROPORTIONATE PRICES.

18, New Bond Street, W.

DIAMOND TIARAS.

1140

1141

1142

1140. Diamond Tiara and to form Necklace £32 10 0
1141. Diamond Tiara and to form Necklace 32 10 0
1142. Diamond Tiara and to form Necklace 485 0 0

A Large Assortment of Diamond Tiaras kept in Stock, Designs of which will be forwarded on Application.

Old Family Jewels Remounted to any design.

THESE DESIGNS ARE DRAWN TO ACTUAL SIZE, AND PRICES ARE QUOTED NET: SMALLER ORNAMENTS OF SAME DESIGN CAN BE HAD AT PROPORTIONATE PRICES.

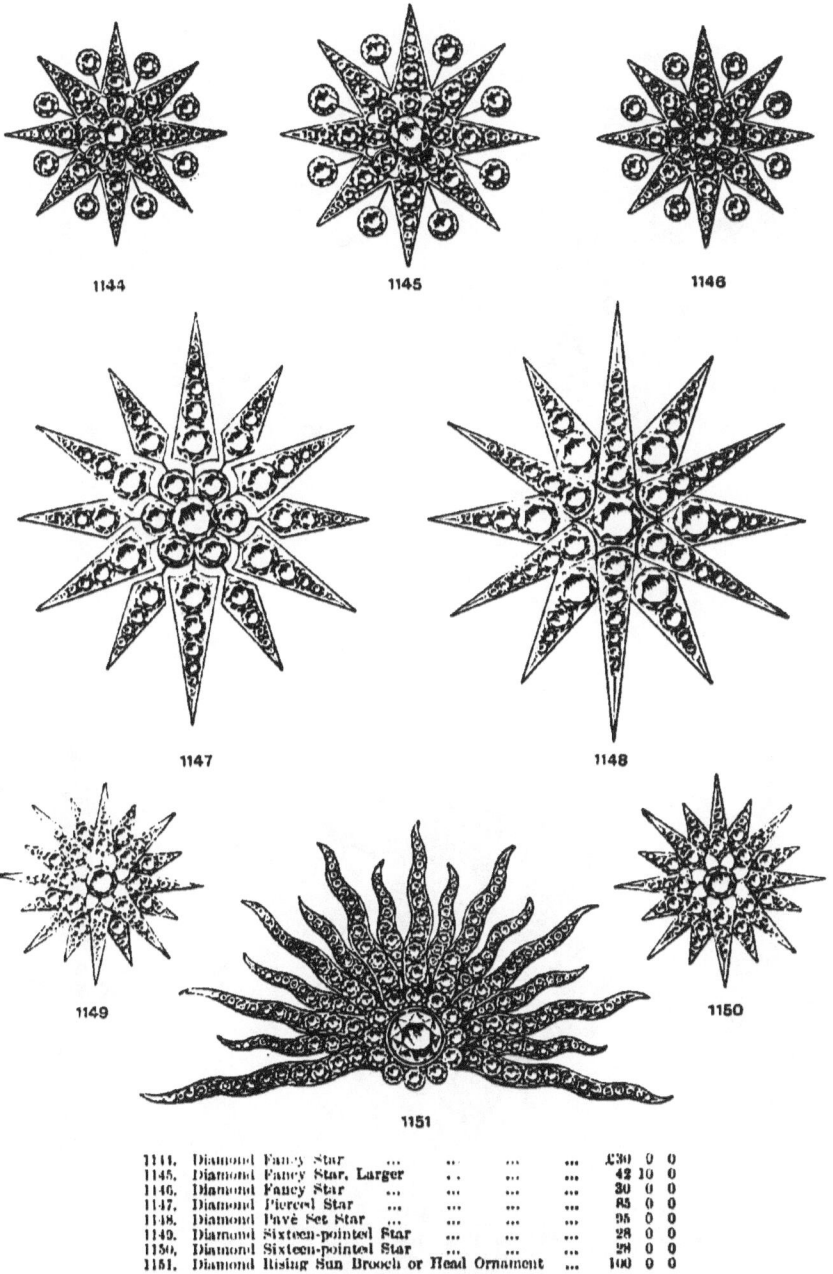

1144   1145   1146

1147   1148

1149   1150

1151

1144.	Diamond Fancy Star	...	...	...	...	£30	0	0
1145.	Diamond Fancy Star, Larger	..	...	...	42	10	0
1146.	Diamond Fancy Star	...	...	...	...	30	0	0
1147.	Diamond Pierced Star	...	...	...	...	85	0	0
1148.	Diamond Pavé Set Star	...	...	...	...	95	0	0
1149.	Diamond Sixteen-pointed Star	...	...	...	28	0	0
1150.	Diamond Sixteen-pointed Star	...	...	...	28	0	0
1151.	Diamond Rising Sun Brooch or Head Ornament	...	100	0	0

THESE DESIGNS ARE DRAWN TO ACTUAL SIZE, AND PRICES ARE QUOTED NET; SMALLER ORNAMENTS OF SAME DESIGN CAN BE HAD AT PROPORTIONATE PRICES.

18, New Bond Street, W.

1152

1153

1154

1155

1156

1152. Diamond Scroll Pattern Comb, will also form Brooch £105 0 0
1153. Diamond Star and Crescent Comb, will also form Brooch 115 0 0
1154. Diamond Arrow Hair Pin and Dress Ornament with Diamond Point ... 60 0 0
1155. Diamond Spike Comb, and to form Brooch 130 0 0
1156. Opal and Diamond Dagger Ornament 10 0 0

THESE DESIGNS ARE DRAWN TO ACTUAL SIZE, AND PRICES ARE QUOTED NET: SMALLER ORNAMENTS OF
SAME DESIGN CAN BE HAD AT PROPORTIONATE PRICES.

STREETER & Co. Ltd.

THESE DESIGNS ARE DRAWN TO ACTUAL SIZE, AND PRICES ARE QUOTED NET; SMALLER ORNAMENTS OF SAME DESIGN CAN BE HAD AT PROPORTIONATE PRICES.

18, New Bond Street, W.

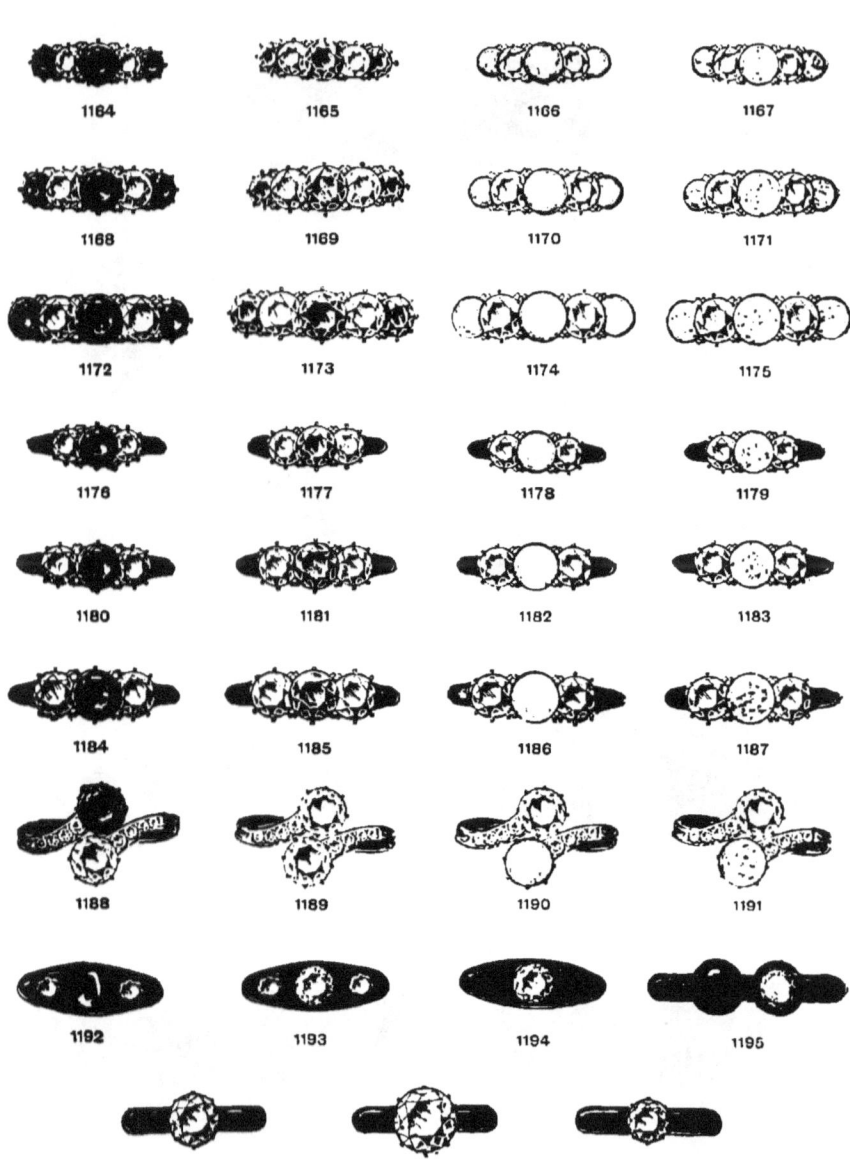

1164   1165   1166   1167

1168   1169   1170   1171

1172   1173   1174   1175

1176   1177   1178   1179

1180   1181   1182   1183

1184   1185   1186   1187

1188   1189   1190   1191

1192   1193   1194   1195

1196   1197   1198

Ruby and Diamond Rings, from £20 to £250.	All Diamond Rings, from £20 to £150.	Turquoise and Diamond Rings, from £12 to £80.	Opal and Diamond Rings, from £12 to £70.

THESE DESIGNS ARE DRAWN TO ACTUAL SIZE, AND PRICES ARE QUOTED NET; SMALLER ORNAMENTS OF SAME DESIGN CAN BE HAD AT PROPORTIONATE PRICES.

STREETER & Co. Ltd.

FINE GEM RINGS.

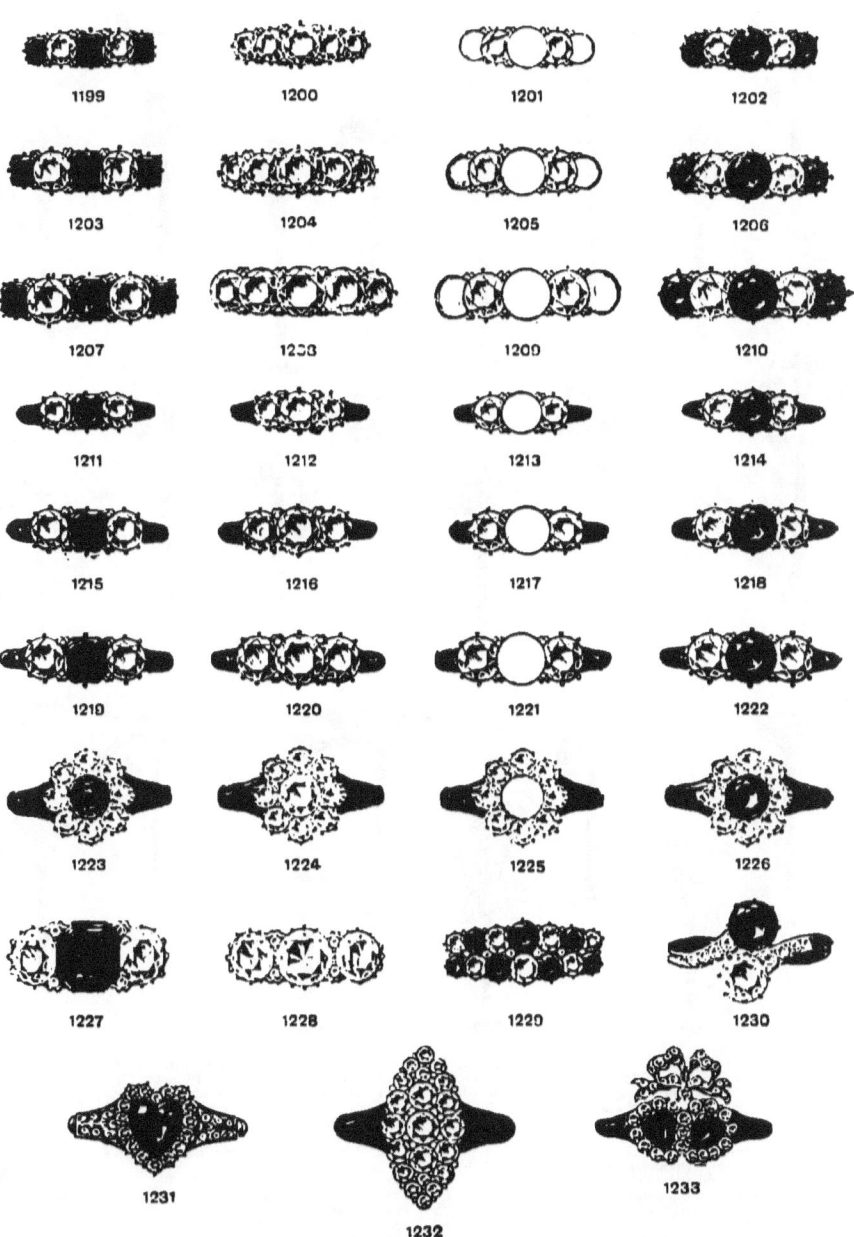

Emerald and Diamond Rings, from £40 to £200.   All Diamond Rings, from £20 to £150.   Pearl and Diamond Rings, from £12 to £200.   Sapphire and Diamond Rings, from £15 to £150.

THESE DESIGNS ARE DRAWN TO ACTUAL SIZE, AND PRICES ARE QUOTED NET; SMALLER ORNAMENTS OF SAME DESIGN CAN BE HAD AT PROPORTIONATE PRICES.

18, New Bond Street, W.

THESE DESIGNS ARE DRAWN TO ACTUAL SIZE, AND PRICES ARE QUOTED NET ; SMALLER ORNAMENTS OF SAME DESIGN CAN BE HAD AT PROPORTIONATE PRICES.

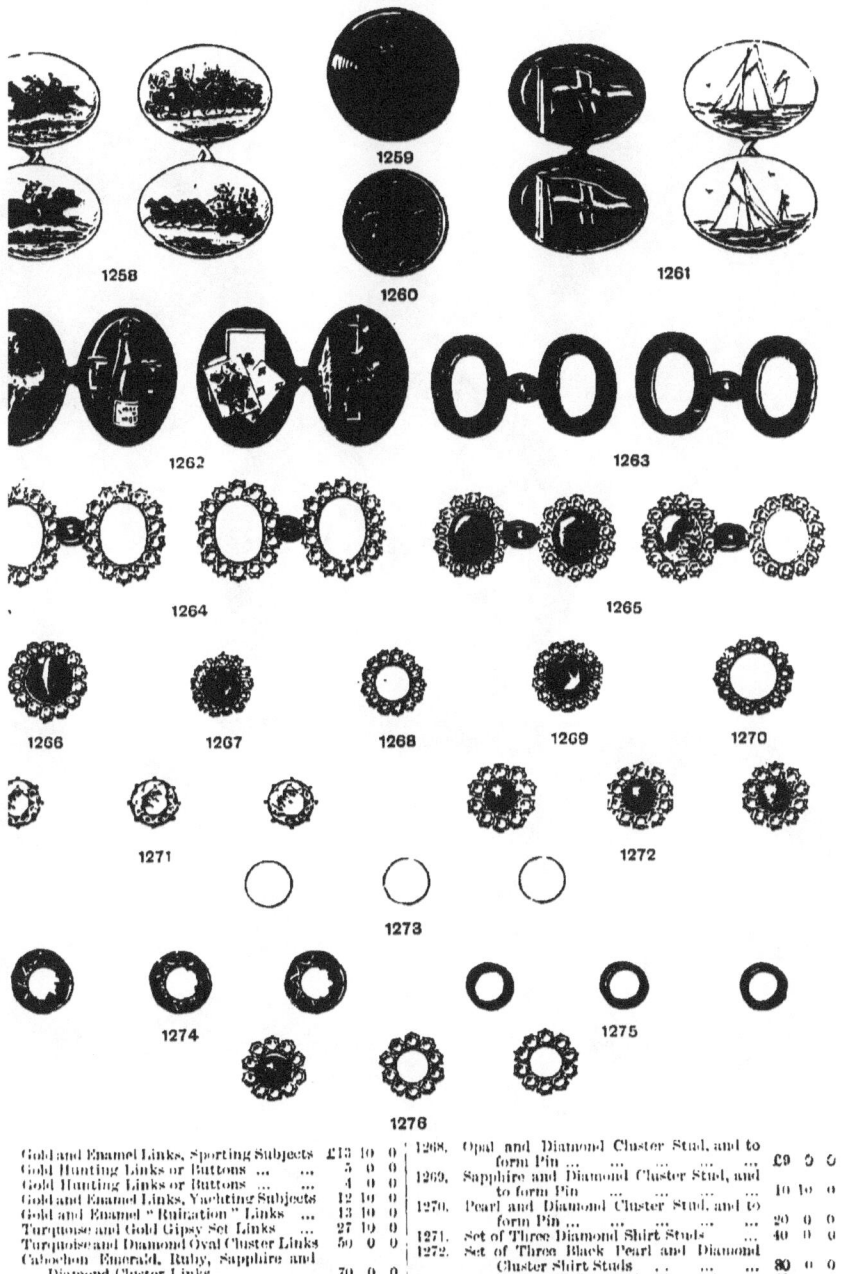

1259

1258

1260

1261

1262

1263

1264

1265

1266   1267   1268   1269   1270

1271   1272

1273

1274   1275

1276

	£ s d			£ s d
Gold and Enamel Links, Sporting Subjects	13 10 0	1268.	Opal and Diamond Cluster Stud, and to form Pin	9 0 0
Gold Hunting Links or Buttons	5 0 0	1269.	Sapphire and Diamond Cluster Stud, and to form Pin	10 10 0
Gold Hunting Links or Buttons	4 0 0	1270.	Pearl and Diamond Cluster Stud, and to form Pin	20 0 0
Gold and Enamel Links, Yachting Subjects	12 10 0	1271.	Set of Three Diamond Shirt Studs	40 0 0
Gold and Enamel " Ruination " Links	13 10 0	1272.	Set of Three Black Pearl and Diamond Cluster Shirt Studs	30 0 0
Turquoise and Gold Gipsy Set Links	27 10 0	1273.	Set of Three White Pearl Shirt Studs	25 0 0
Turquoise and Diamond Oval Cluster Links	50 0 0	1274.	Set of Three Turquoise Star Set Studs	3 10 0
Cabochon Emerald, Ruby, Sapphire and Diamond Cluster Links	70 0 0	1275.	Set of Three Pearl Gipsy Set Studs	4 10 0
Cat's eye and Diamond Cluster Stud, and to form Pin	28 0 0	1276.	Set of Three Pink, Black and White Pearl and Diamond Cluster Studs	55 0 0
Ruby and Diamond Cluster Stud, and to form Pin	10 10 0			

THESE DESIGNS ARE DRAWN TO ACTUAL SIZE, AND PRICES ARE QUOTED NET; SMALLER ORNAMENTS OF SAME DESIGN CAN BE HAD AT PROPORTIONATE PRICES.

Gent's English Keyless Lever Watches, Brequet Sprung, Compensated for Temperatures and Positions, in 18-Carat

Gold Extra Heavy Hunting and Half-Hunting Cases, or with Crystal Face,
from £20.

In Silver Cases, from £8.

STREETER & Co. Ltd.

1282

1283

1284

1285

1286

es' English Keyless Lever Watches, Breguet Sprung, Compensated for Temperatures and Positions, in 18-Carat

Gold Extra Heavy Hunting and Half Hunting Cases, or with Crystal Face,
from £15.

In Silver Cases, from £6 15s.

18, New Bond Street, W.

GENTLEMEN'S CHAINS.

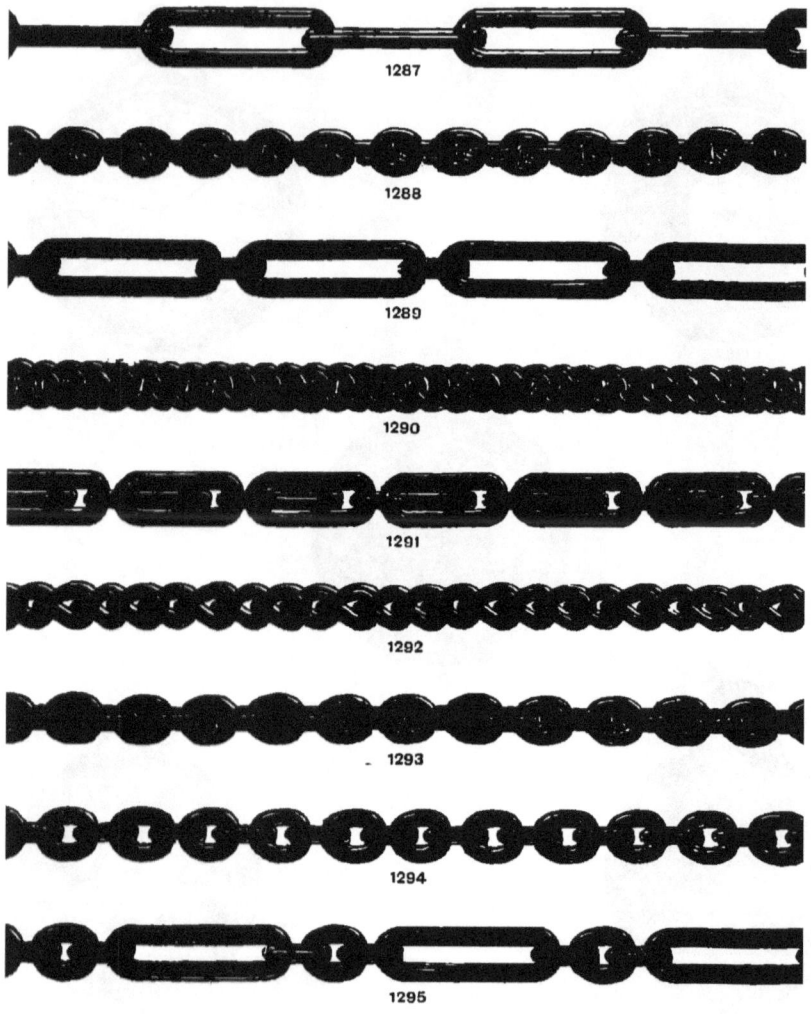

1287

1288

1289

1290

1291

1292

1293

1294

1295

18-Carat Gold Albert and Pocket to Pocket Chains, from £5, according to size.

THESE DESIGNS ARE DRAWN TO ACTUAL SIZE, AND PRICES ARE QUOTED NET; SMALLER ORNAMENTS OF SAME DESIGN CAN BE HAD AT PROPORTIONATE PRICES.

STREETER & Co. Ltd.

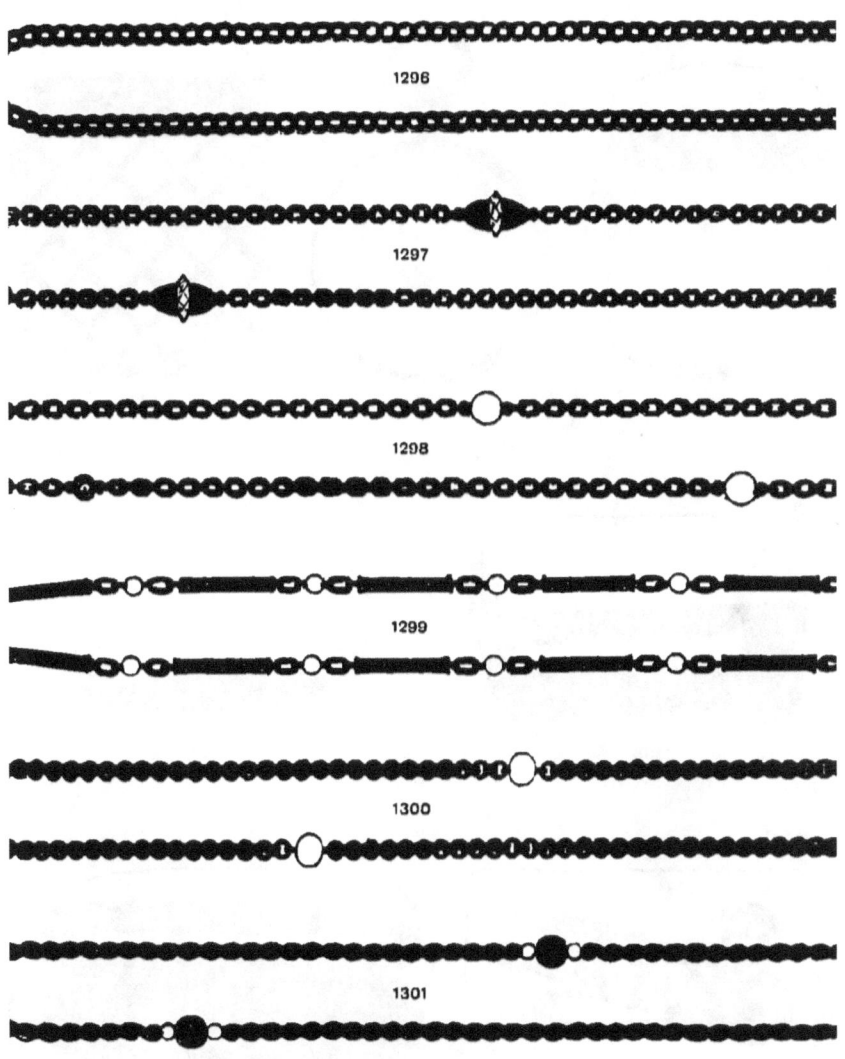

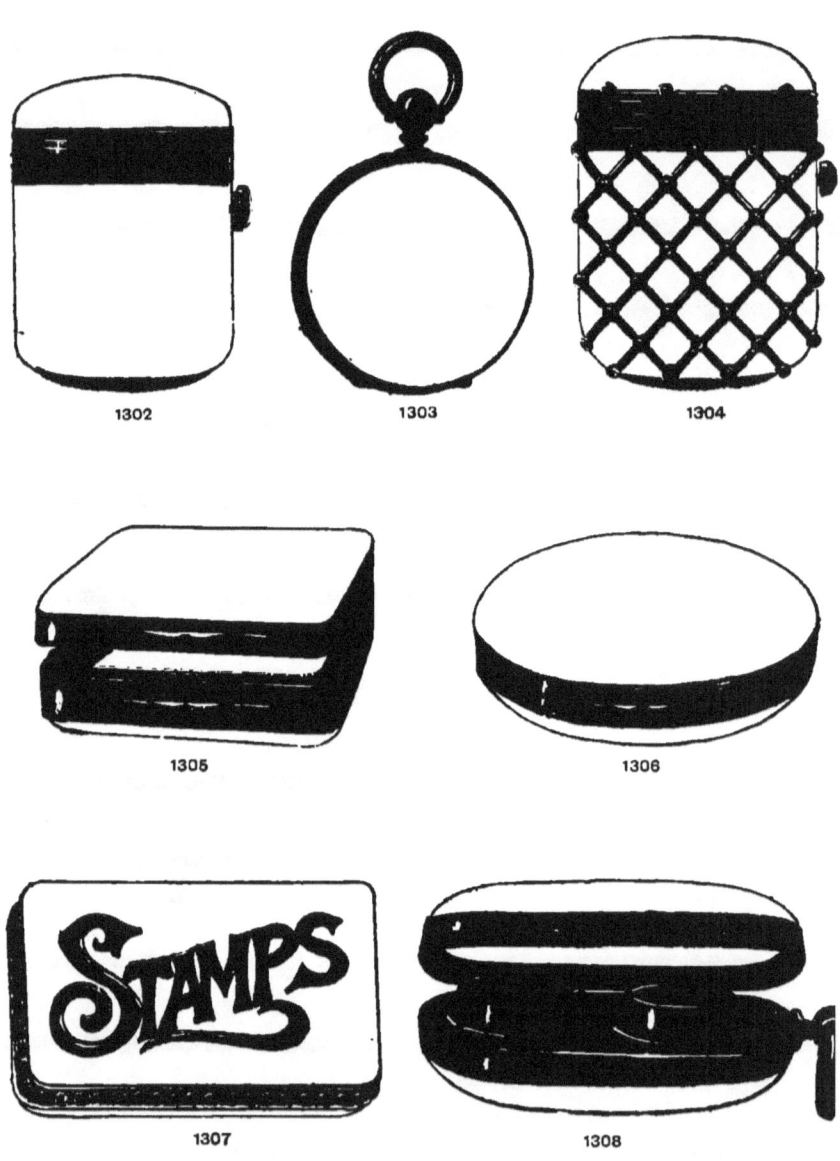

1302   1303   1304

1305   1306

1307   1308

1302,	Gold mounted Amber Match Box, Gem push piece	...	...	...	£8 15 0
1303,	Gold mounted Amber Sovereign Purse	...	...	...	9 0 0
1304,	Gold mounted Amber Match Box, set with Rubies	...	...	...	25 0 0
1305,	Gold mounted Amber Match Box	...	...	...	10 0 0
1306,	Gold mounted Amber Bon-bon Box	...	...	...	6 15 0
1307,	Gold mounted Amber Stamp Box, set with Rubies	...	...	...	22 0 0
1308,	Gold mounted Amber Purse for Sovereigns and Half-Sovereigns	...	...	...	11 11 0

THESE DESIGNS ARE DRAWN TO ACTUAL SIZE, AND PRICES ARE QUOTED NET; SMALLER ORNAMENTS OF SAME DESIGN CAN BE HAD AT PROPORTIONATE PRICES.

STREETER & Co. Ltd.

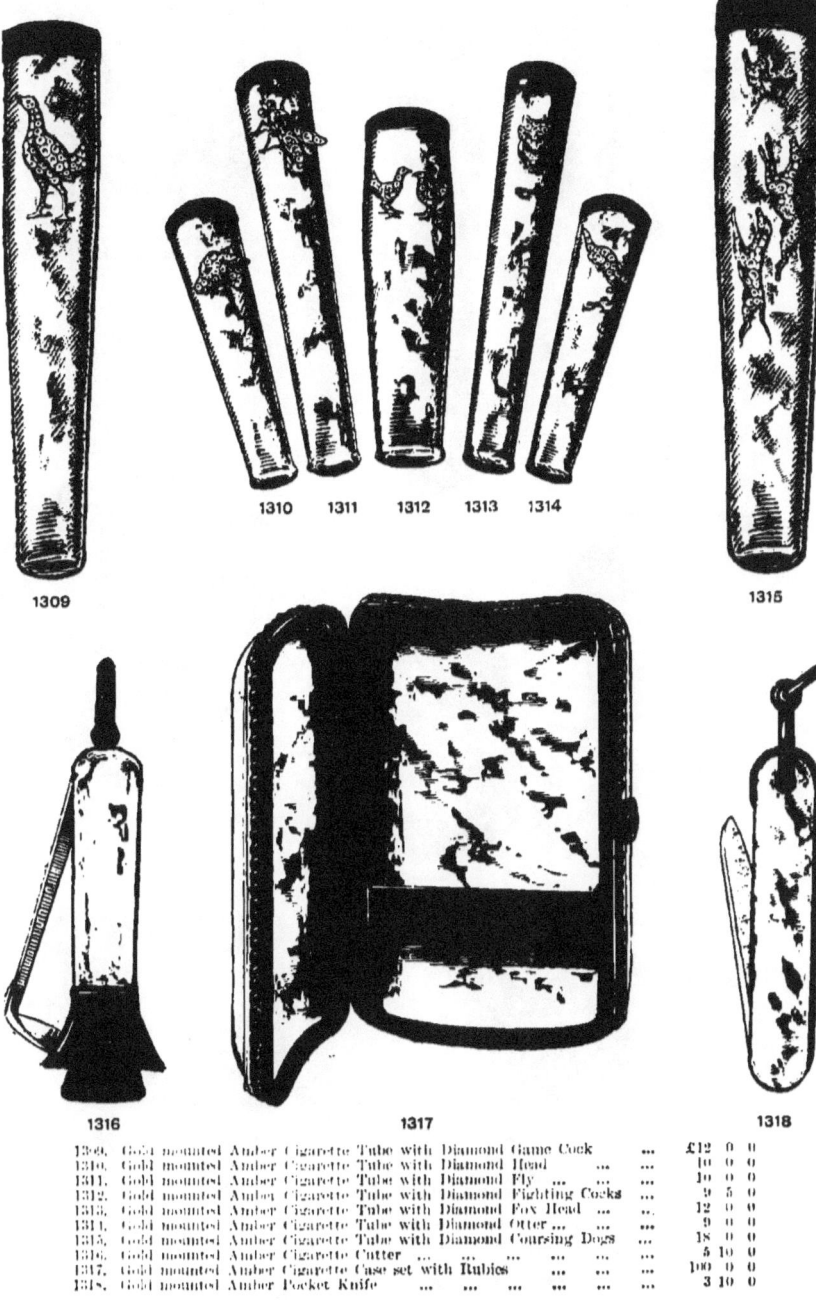

1309   1310   1311   1312   1313   1314   1315

1316   1317   1318

1309. Gold mounted Amber Cigarette Tube with Diamond Game Cock ... £12 0 0
1310. Gold mounted Amber Cigarette Tube with Diamond Head 10 0 0
1311. Gold mounted Amber Cigarette Tube with Diamond Fly 10 0 0
1312. Gold mounted Amber Cigarette Tube with Diamond Fighting Cocks ... 9 5 0
1313. Gold mounted Amber Cigarette Tube with Diamond Fox Head 12 0 0
1314. Gold mounted Amber Cigarette Tube with Diamond Otter 9 0 0
1315. Gold mounted Amber Cigarette Tube with Diamond Coursing Dogs ... 18 0 0
1316. Gold mounted Amber Cigarette Cutter 5 10 0
1317. Gold mounted Amber Cigarette Case set with Rubies 100 0 0
1318. Gold mounted Amber Pocket Knife 3 10 0

THESE DESIGNS ARE DRAWN TO ACTUAL SIZE, AND PRICES ARE QUOTED NET; SMALLER ORNAMENTS OF
SAME DESIGN CAN BE HAD AT PROPORTIONATE PRICES.

18, New Bond Street, W.

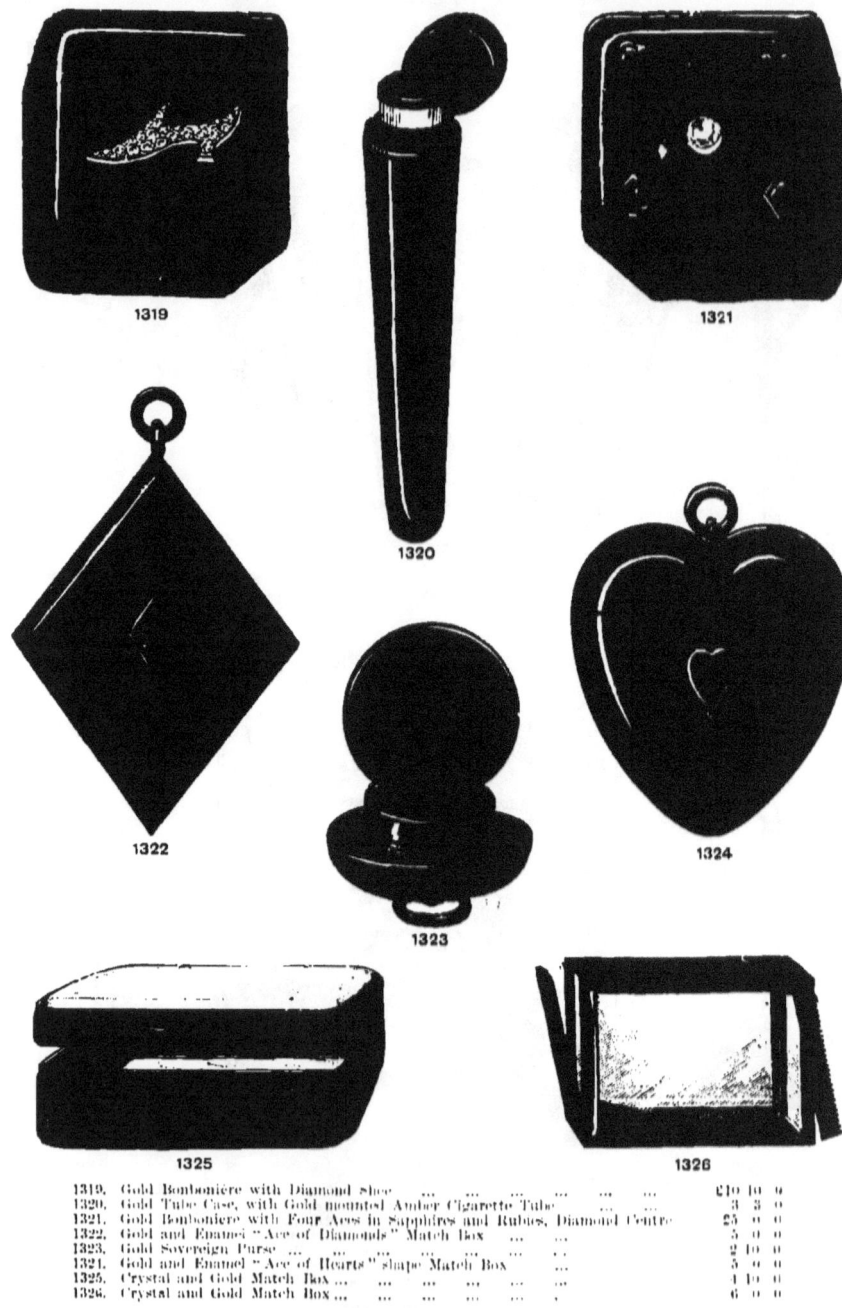

1319   1320   1321

1322   1323   1324

1325   1326

1319. Gold Bomboniere with Diamond Shoe	... ...	£10 10 0
1320. Gold Tube Case, with Gold mounted Amber Cigarette Tube	... ...	3 3 0
1321. Gold Bomboniere with Four Aces in Sapphires and Rubies, Diamond Centre		25 0 0
1322. Gold and Enamel "Ace of Diamonds" Match Box	... ...	5 0 0
1323. Gold Sovereign Purse	... ...	2 10 0
1324. Gold and Enamel "Ace of Hearts" shape Match Box	...	5 0 0
1325. Crystal and Gold Match Box	... ...	4 10 0
1326. Crystal and Gold Match Box	... ...	6 0 0

THESE DESIGNS ARE DRAWN TO ACTUAL SIZE, AND PRICES ARE QUOTED NET; SMALLER ORNAMENTS OF
SAME DESIGN CAN BE HAD AT PROPORTIONATE PRICES,

STREETER & Co. Ltd.

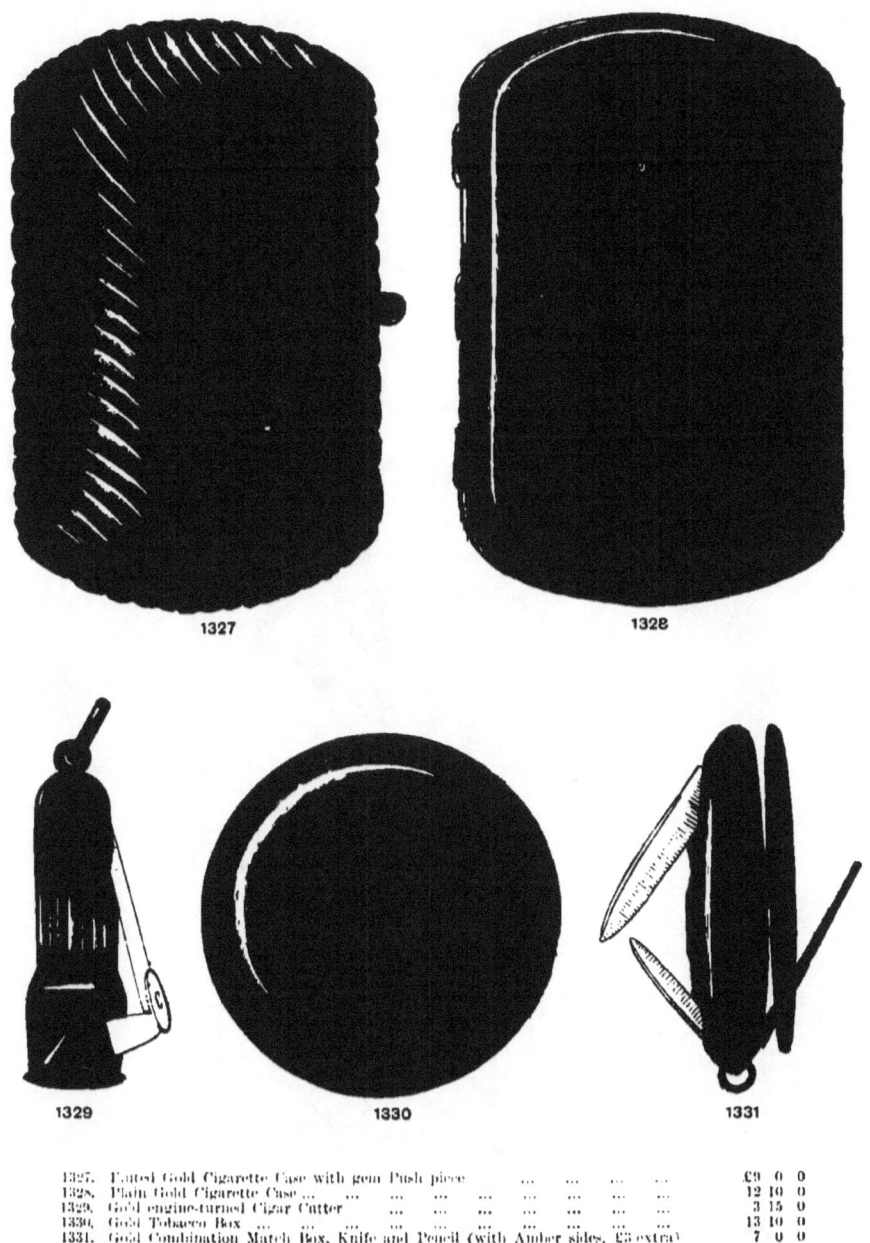

1327

1328

1329

1330

1331

1327. Fluted Gold Cigarette Case with gem Push piece £9 0 0
1328. Plain Gold Cigarette Case 12 10 0
1329. Gold engine-turned Cigar Cutter 3 15 0
1330. Gold Tobacco Box 13 10 0
1331. Gold Combination Match Box, Knife and Pencil (with Amber sides, £3 extra) 7 0 0

THESE DESIGNS ARE DRAWN TO ACTUAL SIZE, AND PRICES ARE QUOTED NET; SMALLER ORNAMENTS OF
SAME DESIGN CAN BE HAD AT PROPORTIONATE PRICES.

44

FERT

NE CEDE MALIS

WARILY

HERALDRY.

———— ⚜ ————

ESSRS. STREETER & CO. having made a special study of Heraldry in all its branches, are enabled to guarantee the correctness of all Armorial bearings with the execution of which they are charged. They have determined to form a special department in order to supervise the correct marshalling and colouring of Arms, which is under the control of Captain F. MANNERS, one of their Directors, who has for years made Heraldry his study.

All branches of this difficult science are included, the Royal Arms (so seldom properly represented), the Badges of Regiments and the Arms of the various Counties and Corporations are given special attention.

MESSRS. STREETER will be glad to furnish Heraldic designs for all purposes—for stained glass windows, internal decorations, carpets, wall papers, note paper, bridesmaids' presents, book-plates, pedigrees, plate, jewellery, flags, fans, ash trays, carriage panels, seals. illuminated addresses, blotting books, or any other purpose.

Their object is to give the public an opportunity of obtaining correct Heraldry without the great expense of referring to the College of Arms on every minor point, feeling sure that their customers will appreciate the advantage of being able to confidently rely on their staff for the strictest accuracy in every detail.

An inspection of their designs is invited in the Museum at 18, New Bond Street.

THE HARDNESS OF GEMS.

T O this property we are indebted for the durability of lustre enjoyed by the gems, in proportion so immensely superior to that of every other natural or artificial product employed as personal ornaments. The lustre of the Diamond may be closely imitated by art ; but the hardness of this stone is a character that defies imitation.

An Austrian mineralogist named Mohs, many years ago suggested a scale of hardness for testing of minerals, which is generally used by mineralogists. At the head of his scale stands the Diamond, and the various degrees are ranged as follows :—

10, Diamond ;

9, Sapphire ;

8, Topaz ;

7, Quartz ;

6, Felspar ;

5. Apatite ;

4, Fluorspar ;

3, Calcite ;

2, Gypsum ;

1, Talc.

To ascertain the hardness of a stone, it is rubbed over an edge of another stone of known hardness. If it scratches, say No. 7, but is scratched by No. 8, its hardness will lie between the two numbers. If it neither scratches nor is scratched by it, the two are identical in degree of hardness. Simple as the test seems to be, it requires considerable skill in some cases to obtain satisfactory results.

To the student of Precious Stones, it is only the first four degrees of hardness that are of interest. It is convenient to have representatives of these mounted in tubes, or handles, for ready use. The Diamond (No. 10) scratches every other stone. The Sapphire (No. 9) stands next in hardness to the Diamond, and scratches all inferior stones. The Topaz (No. 8) and the Rock Crystal (No. 7) are the only other minerals likely to be of service, any substance which can be scratched by Rock Crystal being practically of no value as a Precious Stone. These useful tests are to be obtained of Messrs. STREETER & CO., Ltd., in case complete, as illustrated, of a convenient size to be carried in the waistcoat pocket. Price 21/ .

POCKET CASE OF STONE TESTS,
(Actual Size.)

CONTENTS.

THE TURQUOISE.

 HE Turquoise is a hard gem, of no transparency, yet full of beauty ; its colour is sky-blue, out of a green, in which may be imagined a little milkish infusion.

A clear sky, free from all clouds, will most excellently discover the beauty of a true Turquoise. This gem is throughout of the same beauty, as well internally as externally, its exquisite colour is no doubt owing to the presence of a certain quantity of phosphate of copper. The Turquoise does not occur crystallized, but is found only in a compact form, having no cleavage, but possessing a conchoidal fracture. Chemically, it is a phosphate of alumina, in a hydrated condition. The Shah of Persia has long been credited with the possession of the finest Turquoises in existence, for Nishapur, in Khorassan, the locality from whence the most precious of these stones is obtained, is within his dominions ; and it is said the best Turquoise was invariably picked out and retained by him. The Orientals cut texts from the Koran on Turquoise and fill in the characters with gold. Discoveries in the land of Midian have shown that three Turquoise mines exist there, but all the stones soon lose their colour. It is known that Turquoise was extensively worked by the ancient Mexicans previously to the discovery of America, the stone being highly esteemed for personal ornaments and for the temple of the gods. Turquoise of a green colour is also found in Cochise County, Arizona, at a locality known as Turquoise Mountain, and at a few localities in Nevada and California. Turquoise has also recently been found in great quantities in Victoria.

Chemical composition :—

Phosphorous pentoxide	32.8
Alumina	40.2
Water ...	19.2
Copper oxide	5.3
Iron and Manganese oxides	2.5
	100.0
Hardness	6.
Specific gravity ...	2.75.
Form ...	*Amorphous.*

THE AGATE.

Y the term Agate, the mineralogist understands a composite substance, an association of certain siliceous or quartz-like minerals, which in texture, in colour, and in transparency are diverse one from another. The Agate-forming minerals are chiefly Chalcedony, Carnelian, Jasper, Quartz, and Amethyst. Two or more of these, forming a variegated stone, and usually presenting a diversity of spots and stripes, may be denominated an Agate. The Agate is occasionally found in veins, as in certain localities in Saxony and Bohemia ; although very fine Agates are found in India, our chief supply is derived from South America.

Chemical Composition ...	...	*Silica.*
Hardness ...	...	... 7.
Specific gravity ...	...	... 2.6.
Form ...	...	... *Amorphous, and nodular.*

AMBER

MBER is a fossil resin, and its external condition, as well as its chemical composition, points to its vegetable origin. It is non-crystalline, translucent, and somewhat brittle, having a specific gravity as nearly as possible the same as that of sea-water. It becomes electrical by friction. Amber was much valued by the ancients, particularly by the Romans. It was at one period far more valuable than gold, and although of late years it has been seldom worn as a gem, quite recently there has been a great demand for it in the shape of cigarette cases, match boxes, bonbonières, etc., and it seems as if it is destined to be restored once more to favour.

Composition ...		*Carbon, Hydrogen, and Oxygen*
Specific gravity ...	...	1.08.
Hardness ...	...	2.5.
Form ...	...	*Amorphous, occurring as nodules.*

51

THE AMETHYST.

HIS term is now applied to all the violet and purple crystals of quartz, which, when fractured, present the peculiar rippled or undulated structure described by Sir David Brewster. The stone called Oriental Amethyst is strictly a variety of Sapphire, of violet colour, but the term is applied commercially to any Amethyst of exceptional beauty. Amethyst is a variety of quartz containing traces of oxide of manganese, to which the violet colour of the stone is attributed. Brazil, Uruguay, and Siberia furnish us with the best specimens, but the stone is found in nearly all parts of the world.

Composition	Silica, coloured by oxide of manganese.
Specific gravity	2.6.
Hardness	7.
System of crystallization	Hexagonal.
Forms of crystals	Generally six-sided pyramids and prisms.

THE AQUAMARINE, OR BERYL.

QUAMARINE is a name given to those varieties of Beryl which possess a pale-green colour, suggestive of sea-water. In fact the Beryl, Aquamarine, and Emerald are all united by mineralogists under the head of a single specie, inasmuch as they are found to agree in crystallographic and chemical characters, while they differ mainly in colour. Most of the Aquamarine comes to us from Brazil, but the stones are also found elsewhere, viz.:—In the granite regions of the Ural Mountains, and in Siberia, France, Bavaria, Saxony, Bohemia, in some parts of the United States and in New South Wales.

Composition:—		
Silica	...	66.8
Alumina	...	19.1
Glucina	...	14.1
		100 0
Specific gravity	...	2.7.
Hardness	...	7.5.
System of crystallization	...	Hexagonal.
Forms of crystals	...	Six-sided prisms.

THE BLOODSTONE.

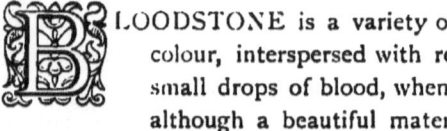 LOODSTONE is a variety of Jasper, of a deep green colour, interspersed with red spots, which resemble small drops of blood, whence its name. Bloodstone, although a beautiful material, is not much used for ornamental purposes, except for signet rings. Being a rather hard stone, and yet not difficult of manipulation, it is a favourite with engravers, and hence crests and monograms are frequently engraved upon it. Cups and other ornamental objects of small size are also fashioned from it.

Composition	*Silica, with a small percentage of peroxide of iron.*
Specific gravity ...	2.6.
Hardness	7.
Form ...	... *Amorphous.*

THE CARNELIAN.

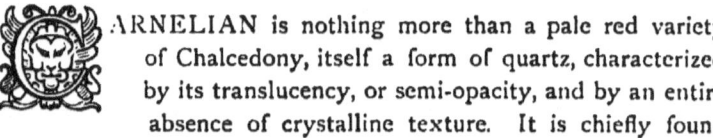 ARNELIAN is nothing more than a pale red variety of Chalcedony, itself a form of quartz, characterized by its translucency, or semi-opacity, and by an entire absence of crystalline texture. It is chiefly found in nodular masses and in the interior of Agates. Its colour varies from blood-red to wax-yellow, and reddish-brown. It is cloudy, seldom striated, semi-transparent, and of waxy lustre. Carnelian is used for rings, seals, beads, etc., and also cameo work and engraving.

Composition ..	*Silica, with oxide of iron.*
Specific gravity	2.6.
Hardness	7.
Form ...	.. *Amorphous.*

THE CHRYSOBERYL.

HERE is probably no stone the composition of which has been given with so much variation as this. The true Chrysoberyl, as known to us to day, is essentially a compound of alumina and glucina, with varying proportions of oxide of iron. There are three varieties of this stone, the Chrysoberyl, the Cymophane or true Oriental Cat's-Eye, and the Alexandrite. Its colours range from light asparagus green, golden yellow, brownish yellow, and golden brown, to columbine red. It is found principally in Ceylon, Brazil, Borneo, and Burmah. Of late years it has also been found in some parts of the United States.

Composition :—*Alumina* ... 78
Glucina ... 18
Ferrous Oxide 4
————
100.

Specific gravity ... 3.5 to 3.8
Hardness 8.5
Crystalline system *Trimetric or ortho-rhombic.*
Form ... ... *Flat prisms, generally as rolled pebbles.*

THE CHRYSOPRASE.

HE true Chrysoprase is a green variety of Chalcedony, of extreme local occurence. It is found in Silesia, not far from Frankenstein. It occurs in veins of serpentine, in company with other siliceous minerals, such as Quartz, Chalcedony, and Opal. Among the semi-precious stones, the Chrysoprase deserves to be one of the greatest favourites. It possesses a beautiful apple-green colour of many shades, and a transparency and capability of high polish. A few seasons ago it sprang suddenly into great favour and the demand was so great that an immense quantity of stained Agate was put upon the market and sold as true Chrysoprase.

Composition :—*Silica* 97.5
Oxide of nickel, &c. ... 2.5
————
100.0
Specific gravity 2.6
Hardness ... 7
Form *Amorphous.*

THE GARNET, CARBUNCLE, AND CINNAMON STONE.

NDER the general name of Garnet, the mineralogist includes a number of stones which present a great variety of colour. On glancing at the various analyses of different Garnets, one might fail to recognise their relationship; but the chemist is aware that these changes of composition take place according to certain definite laws, without violating the general type on which they are constructed. The principal varieties recognised by mineralogists are the Almandine or Precious Garnet; the Essonite, or "Jacinth" and "Hyacinth" the Pyrope, or Bohemian blood-red Garnet, and the Uwarowite, or green Garnet. These all differ slightly in composition, specific gravity, hardness, etc.

Chemical Composition :—

Silica	...	...	36.5
Alumina	...	...	21.0
Iron oxides		...	34.5
Magnesia	...	...	4.0
Lime	...	...	3.0
Manganese oxide	...		1.0
			———
			100.0

Specific gravity	...	...	3.5 *to* 4.3
Hardness	...	...	*About* 7
Crystalline system	...	...	*Cubic*
Forms ...	...	...	*Rhombic, dodecahedron and 24-faced trapezohedron.*

THE HIDDENITE.

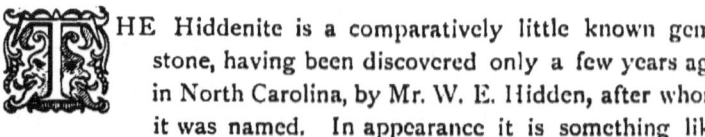

HE Hiddenite is a comparatively little known gem-stone, having been discovered only a few years ago in North Carolina, by Mr. W. E. Hidden, after whom it was named. In appearance it is something like the Emerald, both in its rough and cut states. It is of a brilliant green hue, verging towards yellow, and possesses a beauty of its own. It is a variety of the mineral called Spodumene.

Composition	...	*A silicate of Aluminium and Lithium.*
Specific gravity	...	3.
Hardness	...	7.
Crystalline System		*Monoclinic.*

THE IOLITE.

UNDER the name of Iolite or Dichroite the mineralogist is familiar with a certain stone which is remarkable for its pleochroism, or difference of tint when viewed in different directions. Occasionally it is cut and polished as a gem-stone, and is known to the jeweller as "water Sapphire." The best specimens come from Ceylon, those from Bavaria being almost opaque. The usual colours are various shades of blue and violet.

Chemical composition :—

Silica	...	49
Alumina	...	34
Magnesia	...	9
Ferrous oxide		8
		100

System of Crystallization		*Trimetric.*
Specific gravity	...	2.6
Hardness	...	7.
Form ...	...	*Prismatic crystals, or as pebbles*

JADE.

TRUE Jade is known to mineralogists as Nephrite. It is a compact variety of hornblende, consisting of a silicate of magnesium and calcium. The Chinese have for ages worked this stone into most elaborate and delicate forms. It was also used by the Maories, or natives of New Zealand. It is also found in New Caledonia, Turkestan, Burmah, and a few other localities, in limited quantity.

Chemical composition :—

Silica	...	..	...	57.75
Magnesia	...	...	...	19.86
Lime	...	...	...	14.89
Oxide of Iron, Alumina, &c.				7.50
				100.00

Specific gravity ...	...	...	...		2.91 *to* 3.18
Hardness ...	...	...	...	6.5	
Form ...	...	...	...		*Amorphous ; occuring as a rock.*

JASPER.

Y modern mineralogists the term Jasper is restricted to the opaque varieties of Quartz which present a compact texture, and are destitute of any crystalline structure. Jasper is commonly found in compact masses of kidney shape or as pebbles. Its colours are green, yellow-brown, and red of various shades, rarely blue. Red Jasper is found in Breslau, and in numerous other localities Common Jasper in the old rocks of North Wales and Scotland. Striped Jasper in Siberia, Sicily, Corsica, the Hartz, and Tyrol.

Chemical composition :—

Silica ...	99.5
Oxide of Iron ...	.5
	100.0

Specific gravity	2.6.
Hardness ..	7.
Form ..	*Amorphous.*

LABRADOR.

HIS stone found principally in the Peninsula of Labrador, from whence it takes its name, belongs to the great family of felspars. Generally speaking the body colour is a dull grey, brown, or greenish brown ; but typical specimens of the mineral possess a remarkable iridescent chatoyancy, or internal reflection of prismatic hues, especially bright blue and green, with more or less golden yellow, peach colour, and red. From its remarkable play of colour it has become a great favourite with many connoisseurs, and is much used for cameos.

Composition	*Silicate of aluminium, calcium, and sodium.*
Silica ...	52.9
Alumina ...	29.3
Lime ...	12 3
Soda, etc. ...	5.5
	100.0

Specific gravity ..	2.7.
Hardness	6.
Crystalline System ...	*Triclinic.*
Form	*Usually in cleavable masses.*

LAPIS-LAZULI.

THIS stone is remarkable for its beautiful blue colour, which varies from pale to deep blue, with a tint of green; but is seldom quite pure, being often mottled with white and yellow spots. It is brittle, has but little lustre, and is translucent only at the corners or thin edges. Lapis-Lazuli is found in the Cordilleras, near the sources of the Cazadero and Vias; also in Siberia, in many provinces of China, in Bucharia, and on the banks of the Indus. The stone is used to a limited extent for rings, pins, crosses, etc., as well as for caskets, vases, statuettes, and handles for sticks and umbrellas.

Composition :—Silica	...	...	45.5
Alumina		...	31.8
Soda	...	...	9.1
Lime	...	...	3.5
Iron	...	...	0.8
Sulphuric acid			5.9
Sulphur		.	0.9
Chlorine		...	0.4
Water and loss			2.1
			100.0

Specific gravity	...	...	2.3 *to* 2.5.
Hardness	...	...	5.5.
Crystalline System	...	...	*Isometric.*
Form	...	...	*Dodecahedron, but very rare ; generally massive.*

THE MOONSTONE.

THE Moonstone is an opalescent variety of orthoclase-felspar termed Adularia—a name which it derives from Mount Adula, one of the highest peaks of St. Gothard, where it occurs. The best specimens, however, come from Ceylon. The pleasing lustre of this stone, somewhat like that of mother-of-pearl, has led to its use by the jeweller. Some few seasons ago it found popular favour, too, from being reputed to bring good luck to its possessor.

Silica	...	64.7
Alumina		18.4
Potash	...	16.9
		100.0

Crystalline System	...	*Monoclinic.*
Specific gravity	..	2.5 *to* 2.6.
Hardness	...	6

ORIENTAL ONYX.

NYX is a very celebrated variety of tinted Agate having its colours arranged in parallel strata. The Oriental Onyx is obtained from India, Egypt, Arabia, and Armenia. The inferior variety mostly comes from Uruguay, Bavaria, and Bohemia. The Onyx has been chiefly used for cameos, the figure being carved out of the light colour and standing in relief on the dark ground. By modern mineralogists the term Onyx is restricted to an Agate-like substance, formed of alternating white and brown or black layers of Chalcedony If the strata be alternately white and red, or reddish-brown, the resulting mixture is known as Sardonyx.

Composition ...	...	*Silica, with traces of coloring matter.*
Specific gravity	...	2.6
Hardness ...	...	7.
Form ...	...	*Amorphous.*

THE PERIDOT, OR CHRYSOLITE.

HE Peridot has a very pleasing yellowish-green colour, and is susceptible of a fine polish, but it is so soft as to be easily scratched. It is remarkable that the Peridot occurs in "aerolites" or masses of meteoric stone. Mineralogists include the Chrysolite and the Peridot under the one species Olivine. The colours of Olivine vary from light straw yellow to yellowish green, when the stone receives the name of Chrysolite; and thence to a peculiar soft hue, of a delicate deep yellowish green, when it is called Peridot. It is found in the Levant, in Brazil, Mexico, Arizona, South Africa, and other countries, generally as small pebbles.

Chemical composition :—

Silica ...	39.73
Magnesia ...	50.13
Ferrous oxide	9.19
Nickel oxide, &c.	.95
	100.00

Specific gravity	3.35
Hardness ...	6.5
Crystalline system	*Trimetric.*
Form	*Generally in water-worn pebbles.*

ROCK CRYSTAL.

ROCK CRYSTAL is a pure and limpid form of quartz—a natural variety of silica. It is found in a variety of forms, sometimes of extraordinary size and beauty. Its colour varies from pure white to greyish-white, yellow-white, yellowish-brown, clove-brown, and black. According to its colour it receives a variety of names; thus the yellow is known as false topaz, the brown as cairngorm, and the black as morion. Rock Crystal is now principally used for cameos, intaglios, lenses, spectacles, etc.

Composition—*Oxygen*	...		53.3
Silicon	...		46.7
			———
			100.0

Specific gravity ...	...	...	2.65.
Hardness ..	...	...	7.
Crystalline System	...	...	*Rhombohedral.*
Forms ...	...	...	*Various six-sided prisms,*
			terminating in pyramids.

THE TOPAZ.

UNDER the general name of Topaz modern mineralogists include three distinct stones :—

(1) The true Topaz ;
(2) The yellow Sapphire, or Oriental Topaz ; and
(3) The Occidental, or false Topaz.

The second is a yellow variety of corundum, and the third is nothing but a variety of Scotch quartz. The true Topaz presents a variety of colours, from clear to white, ranging through all shades of light blue and light green to rose pink, orange, and straw yellow. A pink colour is frequently obtained by subjecting the sherry-coloured Topazes to a moderate temperature. It is not uncommonly found in connection with ores of tin in all parts of the world.

Chemical composition—*Alumina*	30.2
Silicon	15.5
Oxygen	36.8
Fluorine	17.5
	———
	100.0

Specific gravity ...		3.5.
Hardness ...	...	...	8.
Crystalline System	...	*Rhombic.*
Form ...	...	...	*Prisms, terminating with pyramids ; the two ends usually dissimilar ; with strongly marked basal cleavage.*

THE TOURMALINE.

EW minerals present greater complexity of chemical constitution than the Tourmaline. Its colours consist of various shades of grey, yellow, blue, pink, and brown; all having a tendency towards the darker hues, even to black. It often happens that the colour is not constant throughout the stone, so that one part may be green while another portion of the same crystal may be decidedly pink. Tourmaline is found in Siberia, Ceylon, the Urals, Saxony, and the Isle of Elba. In the United States it has been discovered in great perfection and abundance.

Composition	...	...	*Very complicated and varied.*
	Silica	...	38.55
	Alumina	...	38.40
	Boron trioxide		7.21
	Ferric oxide	...	5.13
	Ferrous oxide		2.00
	Soda	...	2.37
	Fluorine	...	2.09
	Lithia	...	1.20
	Lime	...	1.14
	Manganic oxide		0.81
	Magnesia	...	0.73
	Potash	...	0.37
			100.00

Specific gravity	...	3.0 *to* 3.15	
Hardness	...	...	7.5
Crystalline system	...	*Rhombohedral.*	
Form	...	...	*Usually in Prisms striated vertically, and differently terminated at opposite ends.*

THE ZIRCON, JARGOON, OR HYACINTH.

HE Zircon, Jargoon, and Hyacinth are all varieties of of the same stone. The term Hyacinth or Jacinth is applied to transparent and bright-coloured varieties; and Jargoon to crystals of dull colour and of a smoky tinge. The Zircon is a lovely stone, the red and brown varieties being especially noteworthy. Some of the finest Jargoons present yellow, green and blue tints, not unlike those of the Tourmaline, but with much more fire and lustre.

Chemical composition—*Silica*		34
	Zirconia	66
		100

Specific gravity	...	4 *to* 4.86.	
Hardness	...	...	7.5.
Crystalline system	...	*Tetragonal.*	
Form	...	...	*Tetragonal prism, with pyramidal terminations; often as rolled pebbles.*

PEARLS.

PEARLS are calcareous concretions formed by certain molluscs, both marine and fresh-water. Most Pearls are obtained from Pearl-Oysters (*Meleagrina Margaritifera*) The chief localities are Ceylon, the Sooloo Archipelago, West Australia, Torres Strait, Gulf of Panama, etc. Fresh-water Pearls are obtained from the Pearl-Mussel (*Unio Margaritifera*), found in the rivers of Scotland, North Wales, Bavaria, Canada, etc,

Composition : From the oyster found in Australian and Ceylonese fisheries. Identical in a sample from each fishery :—

Carbonate of lime	91.72 *per cent.*
Organic matter	59. 4 .,
Water ...	2.25 .,
Loss ...	0.11 ,,

WORKS

BY

EDWIN W. STREETER,

Fellow of the Royal Geographical Society.
Member of the Anthropological Institute.
Gold Medallist of the Royal Order of Frederic.
Holder of a Special Gold Medal from H.M. the King of the Belgian..

———

PRECIOUS STONES AND GEMS.—Demy 8vo. Richly
Illustrated. Cloth, 15/6. Revised and enlarged edition. An exhaustive and
practical work for the merchant, connoisseur, or the private buyer. Treats
upon every description of Precious Stones; giving their history, habitat, value,
and uses for ornament; together with much information regarding their matrix
or rough state, and how to discriminate between the genuine and artificial stones.

CONDITION OF NATIONS.—By G. R. KOLB. Social
and Political; with complete tables of comparative statistics, translated, edited
and collated to 1880, by Dr. and Mrs. BREWER, with original notes and information by EDWIN W. STREETER, F.R.G.S.

GOLD.—(25th Edition). Legal Regulations for the Standard of
Gold of different countries of the World. Coloured tables and facsimiles of
the London and Birmingham hall marks.

THE GREAT DIAMONDS OF THE WORLD.—Their
history and romance. Collected from official, private and other sources during
many years of correspondence and enquiry. The MS. of the " Koh-i-Nur"
graciously read and approved by Her Majesty the Queen. The accounts of the
" Pit" and the " Eugenie" revised by H.I.M. the Empress Eugenie.

PEARLS AND PEARLING LIFE.—Believed to be the only
work published devoted to their history, both ancient and modern. Illustrated

———

GEORGE BELL & SON, YORK ST., COVENT GARDEN.

THE MORNING POST.—" Mr. Streeter prefaces his handsome volume with a warning to his readers that it is not intended as a scientific treatise, but a practical work on the nature, properties, and value of Precious Stones."

THE DAILY CHRONICLE.—" Mr. Streeter brings his wide experience to bear on the subject of Precious Stones. It is the combination of practical ideas with an artistic appreciation of the choicest gems that renders the work interesting."

THE GRAPHIC.—" As a manual of gems ; their market price and characteristics . . . Mr. Streeter's book claims a speciality among the crowd of books on Precious Stones."

THE ART JOURNAL.—" One may read the book for pleasure, and certainly for knowledge."

THE BULLIONIST.—" Is an authority of deserved weight and competence."

THE ILLUSTRATED LONDON NEWS.—" Mr. Streeter, as everybody in London knows, has the best possible reason for being learned about pearls."

VANITY FAIR.—" Mr. Streeter writes as a practical man, and gives us facts and criticisms at first hand."

THE SPECTATOR."—"' Pearls and Pearling Life,' Mr. Streeter has a great deal to say as regards the pearl, both historically and commercially."

THE QUEEN.—" The author who has a fleet ef vessels engaged in the trade has had exceptional opportunities for acquiring information concerning Pearls, and some of his facts are altogether remarkable."

THE STANDARD.—" Mr. Streeter gives an accurate and complete description of every kind of Precious Stone and Gem known, and makes his book still more attractive and complete by a series of coloured plates of several stones in the rough."

THE DAILY TELEGRAPH.—"Considers the knowledge and experience of Mr. Streeter usefully displayed for the information of all."

THE DAILY NEWS.—"Few romances, indeed, can be more entertaining, though the primary object of the volume is strictly of a practical kind."

THE PALL MALL GAZETTE.—"Contains a large amount of information lucidly stated. Of special significance to the admirer of jewels. At once instructive and entertaining."

THE TABLET.—Mr. Streeter has met with great and well-deserved success in his work. It is the outcome of thirty-five years' experience, and the author has spared no pains."

THE WHITEHALL REVIEW.—"Supplies a want which has long been felt. Of singular originality."

THE LEEDS MERCURY.—"The work contains, in a very attractive form, all that is known on the subject."

THE SCOTSMAN.—"Characterises 'Precious Stones and Gems, as an attempt to popularise information on the subject of which it treats."

THE ARMY AND NAVY GAZETTE.—"It would be difficult to enumerate the mass of information."

THE EDINBURGH COURANT.—"Mr. Streeter's subject loses nothing in his hands. He brings to his work both professional knowledge and literary ability."

YORK HERALD.—"A handsome volume . . Useful alike in the library and drawing-room . . . Full of practical hints, research, and historical and descriptive tales."

THE LIVERPOOL DAILY POST.—"It is the work of a recognized authority."

THE SUNDERLAND HERALD.—"This work is well calculated to create increased interest in the subject."

THE GLASGOW HERALD.—"Has never met with a book so satisfying on its particular topic."

HOWLETT & SON, *Printers*, 10, Frith Street, Soho, London, W.

www.ingramcontent.com/pod-product-compliance
Lightning Source LLC
Chambersburg PA
CBHW031246260626
47169CB00007B/2473